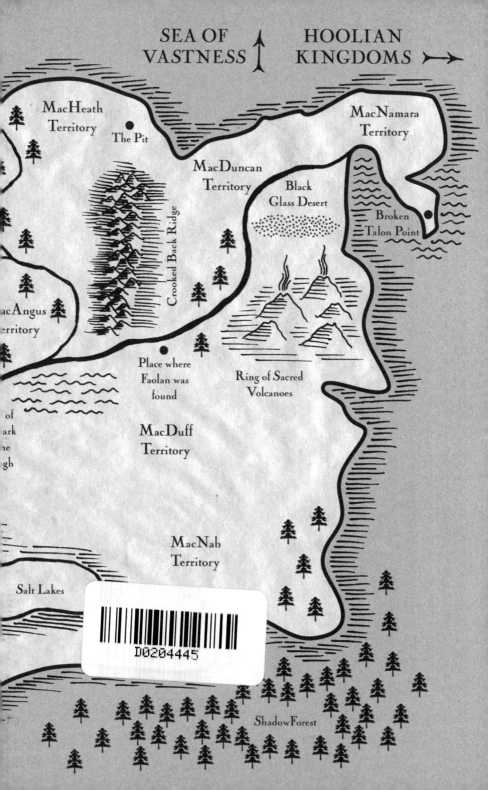

KATHRYN LASKY

WOLVES OF THE BEYOND
WATCH WOLF

SCHOLASTIC PRESS / NEW YORK

Library of Congress Cataloging-in-Publication Data

Lasky, Kathryn.
   Watch wolf / Kathryn Lasky ; [interior illustrations by Richard Cowdrey]. —
1st ed.
      p. cm. — (Wolves of the Beyond ; [3])
   Summary: Faolan, poised to take his place as a member of the revered Wolves
of the Watch, may be the only one who can stop Dunbar MacHeath and his clan
from provoking a war between the Watch and the bears.
   ISBN-13: 978-0-545-09314-9
   ISBN-10: 0-545-09314-7
   [1. Wolves — Fiction. 2. Fantasy.]   I. Cowdrey, Richard, ill.   II. Title.

PZ7.L3274Wat 2011
[Fic] — dc22

                                                        2010049786

10 9 8 7 6 5 4   12 13 14 15

Printed in the U.S.A.   23
First edition, June 2011

Map illustration by Lillie Howard
Book design by Lillie Howard

CONTENTS

PART THREE: THE CUB

PART ONE

THE JOURNEY

THUS SAYETH THE FENGO

TWO WOLVES STOOD ON A WIND-swept bluff overlooking an encampment where, two days before, a contest had been concluded. Faolan, the larger wolf, had a silver pelt and a malformed paw. The second wolf, Edme, was a dusty, rather pathetic-looking creature with one eye. But against the odds, they had won the contest and would now become members of the most elite wolf group in the Beyond — the wolves of the Watch at the Ring of Sacred Volcanoes.

At last, after years of abuse as gnaw wolves, the lowest-ranked wolves of all, they were able to stand tall, their ears shoved forward and their tails stretched high into the wind. But before they traveled to the Ring of Sacred Volcanoes to begin their new lives, there was one last journey to be made. The *Slaan Leat* — the journey of farewell, the journey to make peace. It was a journey toward truth and understanding, toward reconciliation with their fate to be born malformed, a *malcadh*, a cursed one.

All *malcadhs* were cast out of the wolf clans at birth, left to die in the wilderness. Only if they made it back on their own could they win a place with their clan. And they only won honor if they gained a seat on the Watch at the Ring of Sacred Volcanoes. But from the time the first wolves arrived in the Beyond, it was decreed that all gnaw wolves must seek out the *tummfraw* where they were abandoned, before traveling to the Watch. By confronting the place where they were abandoned as pups, they would know that their days of humiliation and desolation as gnaw wolves were finished. Faolan and Edme had each been told the place of their *tummfraw*. Faolan had been abandoned on the banks of the big river that sliced the Beyond in two. For Edme, it was the northernmost peak of Crooked Back Ridge.

A bitter wind cut through the two wolves' pelts. The weather was unseasonably cold for a spring moon, the Moon of the Shedding Antlers. Both wolves looked up. The sky was sealed with roiling storm clouds, as if a blizzard was about to be unleashed. But weather did not concern them as much as this last journey. Through each wolf's mind coursed the same questions. *Will my desolation dissolve? Will I truly find peace? Will I finally belong?*

Their Fengo's words still rang in their ears. *Go forth, find your tummfraws, and know that you are cursed no more. You are malcadhs no more. You are wolves of the Watch and ready to serve. Thus sayeth the first Fengo who led us out of the country of the Long Cold and into the Beyond over one thousand years ago.*

CHAPTER ONE

UNDER THE STARS

"FAOLAN, DID YOU HAVE A SENSE of where your *tummfraw* was before the Fengo told you?" Edme asked.

"Well, I knew it had been on the banks of the river. Thunderheart told me so, but I was never sure where exactly."

"But now that you know, does it seem right?" Edme peered at him intently with her single eye. They had set out together for the first part of their journey since their *tummfraws* were in vaguely the same direction. When the sun rose tomorrow, they would each go separate ways, and then after they had found their *tummfraws*, they would meet up again and travel together to the Ring of Sacred Volcanoes.

"Why do you ask if it seems right, Edme? The Fengo must know."

"I suppose so, but I can't explain it. That peak on Crooked Back Ridge just doesn't seem to fit. I've heard that every gnaw wolf carries a sense of the place they were left to die. That the gnaw wolf has a hunch."

"And you don't?"

"I'm not sure." She paused. "But if I had, it wouldn't be the north peak on the ridge. That just seems entirely wrong to me." She shook her head, as if she was trying to figure out something disturbing.

Faolan looked at her. Their acceptance into the Watch was supposed to mark the end of their desolation and despair, but Edme seemed more hopeless than ever.

Edme was a small wolf. Of all the gnaw wolves, her outward appearance was the most wretched. Yet her bold spirit dispelled pity. She possessed a natural optimism, a good cheer that was all the more remarkable because her clan, the MacHeaths, was known for their brutality. Even now, she tried to muster some of that good cheer, which made Faolan feel sorrier for her.

"Look, Faolan — look at the stars. There's the Great Wolf pointing to the Cave of Souls. Now, what did you say Thunderheart called it?" The question was so like

Edme — full of curiosity, so ready to be interested in someone else and not absorbed in her own worries.

"She said the bears call their Cave of Souls Ursulana."

"What a lovely word — Ursulana." Edme repeated the word as if to savor every syllable.

"I wonder sometimes if all heavens are really one, if there are no borders in the sky."

"Splendid!" Edme exclaimed and began a baying song that she made up as she howled. Long resonant yowls curled into the night as constellations rose in the east, and the blackness of the night tingled with stars. Faolan listened. He hoped — oh, how he hoped — that he was right, that what Edme howled was true, that all those heavens were one. Then someday he would be united with Thunderheart, the grizzly bear who took him in when the wolf clan abandoned him and raised him as her own.

They had camped for the night near a small marsh sprigged with tiny bright yellow blossoms of beewort. The two wolves had found a place to sleep under an outcropping of rock. Across the top of the rock, a spider had woven a web, and its silk threads trembled in the night breeze. Faolan was taken by its delicate beauty. "I've heard that the silk of a spider's web is much stronger than you could ever imagine."

"Really?" Edme's eye sparkled with interest. "Wherever did you hear that, Faolan?"

"The Sark. The Sark of the Slough. She told me. She uses it to stop bleeding and bind wounds."

"You're close to the Sark, aren't you?" Edme asked in a taut voice. Faolan knew that the mere mention of the strange old wolf, whom many regarded as a witch, often provoked this response.

"Yes, she understands me in ways others don't."

"Do you suppose your mother visited her — you know, after . . ." Edme didn't finish the thought, but Faolan knew what she was asking.

After giving birth to a *malcadh* and being cast out of their clans, many she-wolves went to the Sark to recover. She had them drink potions that she brewed to help with what was called the Forgetting, so the she-wolves could move on, find a new clan, a new mate, and birth healthy pups.

"My mother, whoever she was or is, did not visit the Sark. The Sark told me so. Do you think your mother went to her?"

Edme hesitated before answering. "I have no idea, just

as I have no inkling about this *tummfraw*." Faolan noted that Edme did not say "my *tummfraw*." The peak on the ridge had no more meaning for her than the most distant star.

Shortly after the two wolves set off, they picked up a trail of elk headed back north with their young calves. Caribou shed their antlers during the frost moons, but elk shed theirs during the spring moons. Thus this time was called the Moon of the Shedding Antlers or sometimes the Moon of New Antlers.

Mice populations made short work of the antlers, which were rich in nutrients. But Faolan and Edme had found a few still intact and had begun to gnaw them, inscribing them with designs that told the story of their *Slaan Leat*. This desire to gnaw designs was instinctual in Watch wolves. It was not required that they bring a *Slaan Leat* bone back to the Ring. But there was a compulsion that urged them to record their journey. It did not matter if the antler was ever seen or read; they needed to mark this milestone in their journey from gnaw wolf toward a life of service at the Ring of Sacred Volcanoes.

And so they gnawed designs of the constellations floating above them and tried to describe the haunting scent of the beewort that drifted across the marsh, the quivering beauty of the spiderweb sparkling with night dew, and the low, gentle song of the grass as the wind stirred it on this late spring night.

CHAPTER TWO

WINTER DREAMS ON
A SUMMER NIGHT

WHEN THE MOON SLIPPED AWAY,
the wolves fell asleep and huddled against each other
as the night became colder. Faolan dreamed of fire — a
particular fire in the meeting cave of the MacDuncan
clan when he had been brought before the *raghnaid*, the
wolf jury, for having violated hunting law. It was not
the warmth of that bright fire of which he dreamed — a
foil to the cold stares of the jury. It was a pattern of sorts
that flared into his mind, a swirl of bright orange and
yellow buried deep in the base of the flames. The spiraling flame echoed an odd mark on Faolan's splayed paw.
In his dream, the spiral became larger and larger and
seemed to devour him in a spinning madness as the late
chief Duncan MacDuncan's face loomed immense behind
the flames.

"He knew! He knew!"

"Faolan! Wake up!"

Faolan leaped instantly to his feet, towering over Edme. She looked up, concern filling her eyes. "Who knew what?" she asked.

"Did I say something in my sleep?"

"In your dream more likely — a bad dream at that."

"No! No! Not really bad. At least I don't think so. I dreamed of fire, of warmth," Faolan said.

"I dreamed, too, of warmth, a winter dream," Edme replied.

"For a summer vanished. Look!" Faolan peered out from their shelter.

A thin coat of ice skimmed the shallow water of the marsh. To the east, the rising sun splintered on jagged points of grass now stiff with frost.

"What in the world is going on?" Edme said. "Look, the spiderweb is still here, all frosty, and the wind blew hard last night — but there isn't a tear in it! You said it was strong."

"Yes, and you can see that the frost must have doubled its weight. But it's all in one piece."

Edme's teeth were chattering as she stepped close to Faolan. "It's almost the summer moons, the Moon of the Flies. It makes no sense for it to be this cold!"

14

"Those elk and caribou, all the migrating animals, are going to turn right around and head south if this keeps up," Faolan said.

"If this keeps up, it's going to be the hunger moons of winter all year round."

The two wolves, both carrying antlers carved with their *Slaan Leat* stories tucked beneath their chins, parted ways at the edge of the marsh. Faolan was heading farther south toward the river, Edme heading north toward Crooked Back Ridge. They would meet at the beginning of the Moon of the Flies, the first of the true summer moons.

"Let's hope the flies don't become snowflakes," Edme said with a touch of her old familiar cheer, which relieved Faolan. Perhaps she was not as downcast about this *tumm-fraw* business as he had thought. Surely she would feel something when she arrived at her peak.

The sudden frost of the previous night had melted away, and the sun shone bright in the blue bowl of the sky. Edme had expected the ridge to be capped in snow but was surprised at how low the snow line fell. Nevertheless, there was an abundance of tiny flowers flecking the slopes. The flowers that grew at this time of year were called Beyond Blossoms and were known for their toughness and ability to thrive in a harsh land with more rocks than soil and with abrasive winds that scoured away anything that could not cling fiercely. Their blossom time was short, but a night of frost had not discouraged them. Edme paused and set down her antler to study the tiny face of an ice violet. They were the first of the Beyond Blossoms, popping up at the end of the Moon of the Cracking Ice. As she peered into the purple cup with tiny little branching filaments at its center, she marveled at how the flower survived. It was no higher than half the length of one of her claws, and appeared to be growing straight out of the rock. *It's so fragile and yet so strong, like the spiderweb after the frost.*

I must be strong, too, Edme thought as she plodded on toward the crest of the ridge. But with each step forward, she felt an increasing sense of unease. She was anxious, anxious to be done with what she felt was a travesty of some sort regarding this *tummfraw.*

By the time she reached the crest and headed toward the northern peak, it was high noon. *Get it over with,* she told herself. *Just get it over with.* The peak, of course, was not a pointy mountaintop. She knew it wouldn't be. From a distance, all peaks appeared sharp and seemed to prick the sky. But it was just a distortion of perspective. The greater the distance, the sharper the profile of a peak, but when approached, the land flattened. The *tummfraw* loomed up before her now, a flat table rock. She felt nothing. Absolutely nothing. *I was never here — never, ever here. This is not my* tummfraw!

CHAPTER THREE

THE SCENT
OF THE RIVER

THE SCENT OF THE RIVER DOESN'T
change much, no matter the season. Even when the ice is
thick upon it, somehow the river's tang seeps through.
After the Moon of the Cracking Ice in spring, the river
unlocks; the deep ooze of the bottom mud mingles with
the woody fragrance of tree roots that grow on the banks
and are scrubbed by the coursing waters. Faolan felt a
quickening in his marrow as he passed the summer den
and then the spring den where he had spent his infancy
tucked in the embrace of his second Milk Giver, the great
grizzly Thunderheart.

He knew the den as soon as he saw it. There was a
steep embankment and just above it a large cave, where
Thunderheart's last cub had been murdered by a pair of
cougars. Faolan stopped. After all this time, there were

still signs of a skid path down from the higher ground of the cave to the water. Stumps from broken trees stood witness to the grizzly's rage as, wild with grief, she had hurled herself toward the roaring river, only to find that it was too shallow for her to drown. There she had sat for hours, keening into the wind, begging Great Ursus to take her life, until something snagged on her foot. At first she thought it was a clump of river debris torn from the bank in the river's spring tumult. But it was not. It was a tiny wolf pup.

So often Thunderheart had told this story to Faolan. Her words came back to him now as he stood on the spot where Thunderheart had found him, half a league from the *tummfraw* where the Obea Shibaan had left him. He would go to his *tummfraw* soon, but he needed to stop here for a spell and think. *I sought death,* he remembered Thunderheart saying, *and you sought life. You were a gift from the river.* There were no more stories now, for Thunderheart was dead. There were only bones left to gnaw to her memory.

Faolan made his way toward his *tummfraw*. It wasn't as difficult to find as he had thought. He looked down at the bank gouged out now by three winters of rampaging ice and water. A pulse seemed to quiver deep in his marrow, and his hackles rose. This was indeed the place. There was a weathered rut that could have been the very one made when the fragment of ice on which the Obea placed him had torn from the bank. So this was his *tumm-fraw*, this little spot of bank was where, as a mewling pup, he had been left to die.

He circled it three times. There was a familiarity to the spot that stirred the scent glands between the toes of his paws, and he found himself marking the ground. Then he settled on his haunches and looked out at the river flowing gently by. A mist began rising as the river water, still cool from winter, mingled with the warmer air. The mist became thicker, furling and unfurling into undulating patterns that were almost hypnotic. The roar of the river's torrential rampage during the night he was abandoned came back to him. He gripped the banks now as once as a tiny pup he had gripped the ice raft. All of the sensations of those moments came back to him — the dizzying nausea as the ice shelf bounced in the turbulence, the terrible cold when icy water dashed over him, and the roar that grew louder and louder. His claws still digging into the bank, he looked deeply into the mist and saw a familiar pattern. The same design that had swirled through the fire in his dream the previous night now swirled in the mist before him.

In that moment, Faolan knew what he would do. He would bring some of Thunderheart's bones back to the cave high up on the riverbank and build a *drumlyn*, a small mound, to honor her. It had bothered him that he had never seen the *lochin* of Thunderheart climb the star ladders to Ursulana, the bear heaven. If he made this *drumlyn*, it might be a perch from which her spirit could leap. He would build Thunderheart's *drumlyn* not on the place of his abandonment but on the place where he had been found. This was the meaning of the *Slaan Leat* for him. The mist had cleared and the river ran on smooth and dark, like an amber ribbon. As Faolan trotted at a brisk pace toward the secret place where he had buried the bones of his second Milk Giver, another thought began to seep into his mind as if out of nowhere. *My first Milk Giver! Who was she? What did she think of me? Did she feel cursed to give birth to such a pup? Were there others? Do I have sisters or brothers still in the clan?*

CHAPTER FOUR

A TRUE GNAW WOLF?

AS EDME MADE HER WAY DOWN from the northern peak of Crooked Back Ridge, she could not help but wonder what Faolan had felt when he found his *tummfraw*. She was certain that he would not have experienced the same emptiness she had when she stepped onto the table rock at the peak. Whenever she thought about it, she wanted to blame herself, but she knew this made no sense. She was not to blame — if anything, it was the *tummfraw* that was wrong, or the Fengo who had made a mistake. She was almost tempted to go to the Obea of the MacHeath clan and ask her point-blank if this was the right *tummfraw*. But Edme had to be honest with herself. She loathed the entire clan and had no desire to go back into MacHeath territory.

The MacHeath Obea was a white wolf named Airmead. This was a cruel name, for in the Old Wolf language, it meant "barren." Of course all Obeas were barren, but only the MacHeaths would choose to take away whatever the Obea's real name was to call her after her pathetic condition. The MacHeaths had a malevolent instinct that flowed through their blood like a treacherous current. They fed off it like vampire bats drink blood from animals, leaving just enough to ensure that the animals live and the bat can come back for more. MacHeaths who did not feed off cruelty either grew weak and died or left for one of two places — west to the Outermost to live with the savage outclanners, or far to the northeast to the MacNamara clan. No, Edme had no desire to see any of the MacHeaths. She was already too close to their territory for comfort.

As she wound her way down and across the steep slopes of the ridge, Edme tried to imagine how a little one-eyed pup could have made her way down the precipitous slope and back to her clan. They said that all *malcadhs* who survived had an instinct that led them back to their clan's territory. But Edme found it hard to believe. Her urge had always been to put as much distance as possible between herself and her clan.

She was still occupied with these thoughts when she reached the bottom of the ridge, and a pair of yearlings, Ingliss and Kyran, from the chieftain's pack of the MacHeath clan appeared. She felt a twitch deep in her marrow. These two young females had particularly enjoyed abusing her when she was a gnaw wolf. They knew exactly where to attack to cause her the most fear as well as the most pain, and took pleasure in biting her as close as they could to her one good eye. She instinctively lowered her tail and began to sink into a submission posture, but suddenly stopped. *I don't need to do this anymore. I am not a gnaw wolf. I am a member of the Watch. If anything, they should submit to me.* Edme's hackles raised, she shoved her ears forward, and her single eye glinted bright green.

"Well, you've certainly learned quickly!" Ingliss, the larger of the two, said.

"Yes, but doesn't a one-eyed wolf look funny with her hackles up?" Kyran added nastily. Kyran always took her cues from Ingliss. They worked as a tag team of abuse.

"You know, of course, you don't deserve to go to the Ring," Ingliss said. Edme tilted her head. She wouldn't deign to answer them and walked on. But they followed her, one on either side, pressing close.

"Get away!" Edme yipped. "You can't do this to me anymore, either with words or bites."

"Oh, yes, that's true," Ingliss said brightly. "Indeed we should never have abused you. Seeing as you were never a true gnaw wolf."

This stopped Edme. "Are you *cag mag*? What are you talking about?"

"Wouldn't you like to know?" Ingliss teased. She turned to Kyran. "Should we tell her?"

"I suppose so," Kyran replied casually, as if she had better things on her mind.

"Dear Edme, we have come to apologize for our behavior," Ingliss said. Edme's head swiveled between the two wolves.

Edme tried desperately to maintain a cool, disinterested demeanor. "An apology is not necessary, really. Now on your way. I must get to the Ring and the Watch."

"I wouldn't rush if I were you," Kyran said.

"No, no, definitely not. For what will they say when they discover you were not born a *malcadh*, but made one!"

"What are you talking about?" Edme said, and she bared her teeth. Never had such a small wolf seemed so fierce.

The two yearlings cowered. "He did it to you, the chieftain Dunbar MacHeath!" Kyran blurted.

"Did what?"

"Tore out your eye!" Ingliss said.

"You mean . . . you mean . . ." Edme's jaw dropped open. It was as if she was searching for the actual words. "I wasn't born this way?"

"Not at all," the two wolves said at once, regaining their composure. A smirk crawled across Ingliss's face. "We heard it whispered in the *gadderheal*. So you see, you are not a true gnaw wolf," Ingliss said.

"You're a fake," Kyran offered. "They'll reject you when they find out."

"They sense these things," Ingliss said.

"What if I tell them?" Edme said, turning around and heading straight into the heart of MacHeath territory.

"Tell them? Tell who? Where are you going, Edme?"

"To your chieftain."

"What?" the two wolves shrieked.

"You're telling him what we told you? We'll get in big trouble!" Ingliss was running beside Edme now, pleading with her.

"You should have thought of that before."

"But what's the use of telling Dunbar MacHeath? What will you tell him exactly?"

"Exactly?" Edme stopped short, and the beam from her single eye seemed to pierce Ingliss right to her marrow. "I shall tell him that I will serve at the Ring not as a member of the MacHeath clan, but as a free runner!"

26

The two yearlings collapsed and began crawling after Edme on their bellies, begging her not to go to the chieftain. But Edme closed her ears and trotted on toward the Carreg Gaer of the MacHeath clan. Now it all made sense. She felt nothing when she arrived at her *tummfraw* because she had no connection with it whatsoever. Had they gone through the rituals of kicking out her birth mother and sire from the clan? What did it matter? It was all a charade and nothing more.

But she had not endured this life of violent abuse for nothing, nor had the *gaddergnaw* in which she had competed been for nothing. She had won that contest fair and square. She might not have been born a *malcadh*, but she was a true member of the Watch. She would serve honestly, although her origins were not honest. She would serve courageously, although for most of her life she had cowered in the shadows of intimidation. Deep, deep within her marrow, Edme knew that she was meant to be a wolf of the Watch.

While Edme was heading for the MacHeath clan, Faolan was dragging Thunderheart's immense femur from where she had died to the place where she had first found Faolan and become his second Milk Giver.

Thunderheart had been killed in an earthquake when Faolan was barely a year old. A gigantic boulder had rolled down on her, knocking her senseless. There she must have lain, bleeding to death. When he had first come upon her huge skull a few moons after her death, it loomed immense and pure white in the moonlight. But now, after two years, new life had taken root in it. Mosses and lichen crept over the cranium and down her long muzzle. And out of one eye popped a small constellation of starflowers. There was no way that Faolan could move her skull, nor did he want to. The skull itself had become a memorial to life. But he did transport as many of the smaller bones as he could. The *drumlyn* he would make would not stand simply as a tribute to life but to Thunderheart's afterlife in Ursulana.

Faolan wondered if Thunderheart had traveled to Ursulana. He knew she had died, but her spirit seemed to linger on earth. Did she have unfinished business? His friend Gwynneth, a Masked Owl, had told him it was that way with the scrooms of dead owls. They would not seek Glaumora in earnest until their business on earth was complete. By building this *drumlyn*, Faolan hoped to give Thunderheart's spirit, or what wolves called her *lochin*, a sign. The *drumlyn* would declare that he, Faolan, was fine, that Thunderheart could cease her watch on earth. He had already carved the story of their life together on a paw bone he had retrieved soon after he had found her skeleton. He didn't need to carve any more. The moment he placed Thunderheart's femur on top of the paw bone he had incised so beautifully, it was as if a weight had shifted somewhere within Faolan's chest. He looked up as the stars broke out, and began to howl:

> *Thunderheart*
> *Go away*
> *Shut your eyes on this earth*
> *The time has come*
> *Leave your bones behind*
> *Climb high, then higher*
> *On the star rungs*
> *Claw your way to Ursulana*
> *That's where you should go*
> *How I do long to look to the sky*
> *And see your deep glow*
> *Among the stars that rise in the night*
> *Go now, go now, join that constellation so bright*
> *There is nothing left for you here*
> *And know that your son has nothing to fear*

Though the pangs of your death
Leave me forever stunned
The taste of your milk is still sweet on my tongue
The huge paws that cradled me
Never betrayed me
But held me so close to your breast
That the beat of your massive heart
Still echoes within my own chest
Oh, Thunderheart, Thunderheart,
Time to go away.

CHAPTER FIVE

BLOOD AND THORNS

ON THE CUSP OF SUMMER, WHEN the earth begins to tilt more steeply toward the sun, there is a day when the sun and the moon hang side by side in the sky. It is on this single day and night when the Litha blossoms in the Beyond. The tiny red roses tip their faces toward the radiant sun and her softly glowing sister, the moon, from which they gather their nourishment.

The Litha blossoms are the deepest red and their thorns are as sharp as wolf fangs. The leaves of the Litha are succulent, with a juice strong enough to make a wolf tipsy. However, to get past the thorns to the spirited grog of the leaves is an uncomfortable task at best. Although the appearance of the roses marks the longest day of the year, it also signals the turn of the earth toward winter, for in the warm days after, the sun will slip below the horizon a bit earlier and a sliver of daylight will disappear as the shadows of evening advance more quickly. The night the Litha appears is called the eve of Blood and Thorns and there are rowdy celebrations in all the packs of all the clans in the Beyond. None celebrate Litha Eve more exuberantly than the MacHeath clan, often with disastrous conclusions as some wolf gets killed in what was supposed to be a "friendly" wrestling match.

As a gnaw wolf in the MacHeath chieftain's pack, Edme had made herself scarce on Litha Eve, but now as she entered the encampment, the howls and baying that had scored the air dwindled, and she felt a silence fall in behind her. The wolves of the pack stared in utter dismay as Edme returned with her tail lifted high and her ears shoved forward. A grimace of aggression scored her face as she moved toward the *gadderheal*, the ceremonial cave of the chieftain's pack. She heard low growling whispers as she drew near.

"What's she doing, going to the *gadderheal*?"

"On Litha Eve?"

"Look at her tail and ears. She certainly learned the dominance postures quickly."

"Well, by my marrow, I'll not scrape to her!"

Edme heard the last remark and could only laugh to

herself. *By tomorrow or sooner, you'll come begging. But I'll be gone, gone to the Ring as a free runner.*

"Free runner" was the term for a gnaw wolf who was born clanless in the wild and left to die by its mother. Free runners were permitted to compete in the *gadder-gnaw*, and if they proved themselves, they could be selected for the Watch at the Ring of Sacred Volcanoes. Edme had always felt that Faolan was essentially a free runner because he had not found his way back to the MacDuncan clan until well past his first year. She fully intended to declare herself first to the MacHeath clan as a free runner and then to the Fengo. The *Slaan Leat* was a journey toward truth, a journey toward peace. Well, she had found her truth and her peace, and so had completed her task.

As Edme drew toward the entrance of the *gadderheal*, she saw the chieftain Dunbar MacHeath staggering to his feet with the aid of one of his sublieutenants. A scar ran diagonally down his face from the edge of one eye all the way to his neck, where no fur grew. The exposed skin of the scar was puckered and raw, giving him an especially savage look. Although now, swaying unsteadily and mostly supported by his sublieutenant, the chieftain simply looked ridiculous. His muzzle was thick with his own blood, from his attempts to get at the Litha leaves. He had apparently succeeded, for he was quite drunk. Edme guessed that he would sober up quickly when she announced the reason for her visit.

"What in the name of the dim world are you doing here, cursed one?" he snarled. "Did they reject you already?"

"It's not a question of their rejection, but mine."

"What's she saying?" The chieftain turned to his lieutenant and then vomited on the ground.

Edme's hackles rose so high, they made her look larger than she had ever seemed. The beam of green light from her one eye grew more intense, and Dunbar MacHeath and his lieutenant averted their gazes as one might shift one's eyes during a solar eclipse when the pinpoint needle of the sun becomes blinding.

"Step into the *gadderheal* and call your *raghnaid*, if you please."

Dunbar MacHeath suddenly stood erect, but his tail drooped in a half-submissive posture. His lieutenant went around to his hindquarters and flicked his tail as a reminder to Dunbar not to cower. Edme led the way into the *gadderheal*.

I can't quite believe this, she thought. It was as if the whole world had tilted on its axis. She was leading the chieftain into his own ceremonial cave. She was commanding him, or so it seemed, on this Litha Eve.

Fewer than a dozen wolves in varying states of inebriation entered the *gadderheal*. They glanced first at Edme, for she suddenly seemed transformed. Yes, it was the same small wolf with the same mangled face, missing one eye. But with her hackles up and her tail raised, she appeared larger. And when they glanced at their chieftain, he seemed somehow slighter. His pelt, prickly with thorns and streaked in his own blood from his assaults on the Litha rose, appeared to have shrunk and to cling to his bones. He had assumed all the postures of dominance, but it seemed a bit of a joke, as if he were a little pup trying them for the first time. Airmead the Obea slipped into the *gadderheal*. With her pure white pelt unstained by Litha grog, she seemed no more than a scrap of fog blown in on a breeze.

Trying to muster all the dignity he could, Dunbar MacHeath stepped toward Edme. "Why have you returned if the Fengo of the Watch has not rejected you?"

"Why do you jump to the conclusion that the Fengo has rejected me? Is there reason that he should?" Edme let the question hang in the air, which had become quite chilly for Litha Eve.

"No! No, of course not!"

The chieftain does protest too vigorously, Edme thought. She nodded with just a hint of submission. "I was born a poor *malcadh*, was I not?" She turned to the Obea, whom no one had yet noticed.

Dunbar spoke up now. "Yes, come forth, Airmead. You were the one who took this *malcadh* to the *tummfraw*. Will you not testify to that?"

"I would prefer not to, my lord."

"It's not a matter of preference!" Dunbar MacHeath growled and walked up to the Obea stiff-legged, grabbing her by the ruff of her neck and flinging her to the ground.

"No need to abuse the Obea!" Edme rammed the chieftain with her head, throwing him off balance though he was twice her size. "I know my story. I was not born a *malcadh* but a *malcadh* made! Who was it who tore out my eye? You, Dunbar?"

There was a gasp. Never had a wolf challenged a chieftain so blatantly. Edme had head-butted Dunbar MacHeath and, almost worse, addressed him without title, by his first name.

"Who told you this?" Dunbar MacHeath said through clenched teeth. "Who told you?"

"Who told me doesn't matter. But listen carefully." The tension in the cave thickened. Edme sensed that she was teetering on a dangerous edge as more wolves, many very drunk, made their way into the *gadderheal*. Some of these wolves were members of the *raghnaid*, the clan court that interpreted the complex laws of the wolves of the Beyond. All of them bore a dusting of snow that mixed with the streaks of blood on their muzzles. *How strange this weather is. Snowing on Litha Eve — unheard of!* thought Edme. It gave her an idea. She would play on the deep superstition that all the wolves harbored, but in particular the wolves of the MacHeath and the MacDuff clans.

She continued speaking. "Hear what I have to say. This weather is strange, is it not? Perhaps not since the Ice March have wolves been seen with snow on them in this moon." She nodded toward the wolves who had just entered the cave.

"Very strange," said a wolf named Blyden. "Weather's gone a bit *cag mag*, I'd say!"

"Shut up," barked the chieftain.

Edme nodded at Blyden as if he were the most intelligent wolf in the cave, which he definitely was not. The slender ash-colored wolf was very strong and had savage fangs, always good for a fight or one of the kill squads known as *slink melfs*. These squads were specifically formed to bring down any animal who endangered the clan.

Edme began to speak again and affected a grave but considered air, as if she were turning something over in her mind. "You don't suppose the *cag maggish* turn is because of your deceit? I ask you, distinguished members of the *raghnaid*, to ponder how the laws pertaining to *malcadhs* have been broken. Ripping out a pup's eye so that she might become a member of the Watch! Could you have offended the spirit of that first Fengo who led us out of the Long Cold on the Ice March? Perhaps that explains this turn of weather."

There were gasps and strangled little mewlings, as if a milk pup had been deprived of a teat. For though violence streamed through the MacHeaths' blood, cowardice was lodged deep in their marrow. Edme stepped closer to the *raghnaid* members. What a joke they were, compared to the *raghnaids* of clans such as the MacDuncans, the MacNabs, or the MacAnguses.

"I will go to the Ring of Sacred Volcanoes, but I shall go not as a member of the MacHeath clan — no, I shall go as a free runner. I reject you. I deny you, I refuse and repudiate you as my clan."

Confusion swam in Dunbar MacHeath's eyes, his jaw

hung open in disbelief, and threads of saliva, stained deep magenta from the Litha grog, fell to the floor of the *gadderheal*. Edme turned and left before the MacHeath wolves could grasp what she had said. By the time her words sunk in, Edme was gone.

The world swirled with snow. A blizzard! A blizzard on Litha Eve and the beginning of the summer moons!

A clamor broke out in the *gadderheal*.

"Kill her!" someone howled.

"Tear out her other eye!" said another.

"No, rip out her tongue so she can't speak!"

Dunbar MacHeath barked the command for silence. He had regained his wits and now assumed a baleful and terrifying demeanor. Every hair in his pelt bristled until he looked twice his normal size.

"Listen to me, wolves of the MacHeath clan. Listen to your chieftain. There will be no killing" — Dunbar paused dramatically and eyed his sublieutenants — "until I say so." Again he paused. "But when the time comes, there is going to be something worse than death for the traitorous wolf Edme. Far worse than mere murder!"

"What's worse than murder?"

"We shall watch her carefully."

The lieutenants exchanged uncertain glances, as if to say, *Watching her? That's worse than killing?* For in their small minds, pinched by violence, it was hard to imagine alternatives that did not involve bloodletting.

The chieftain continued, "We shall watch her and find her weakness, and when we do, then the punishment will begin."

The chieftain shook with fury. He had waited too long for the MacHeaths to have a member of the clan on the Sacred Watch. *But why stop there?* A new idea began to brew in Dunbar's quickly sobering brain. The chieftain felt a shiver of excitement pass through the assembled wolves. He waited and let several seconds pass. If there was one talent that Dunbar MacHeath possessed, it was the gift of manipulation. He spoke his next words so quietly that every wolf had to strain to hear them.

"My friends, you might just be looking at the next Fengo."

There was a collective gasp followed by a long hush.

CHAPTER SIX

THE OBEA SPEAKS

WITHIN THE WHITENESS OF THE swirling blizzard was an even brighter patch at the center of the spinning frenzy of snow. The Obea had followed Edme into the storm. She now began to howl, "Stop, Edme. Stop! It's me, Airmead!"

The very name split the fury of the storm. Seldom was an Obea's name spoken out loud, and it was unthinkable that an Obea would refer to herself by her given name. If gnaw wolves were the lowest-ranked wolves in a clan and the objects of physical and verbal abuse, Obeas were wolves of no rank at all. They were barren, and existed in a social purgatory that was beneath the contempt of any wolf in the clan, almost as if the Obeas were invisible. Airmead had heard that in other clans this purgatory was not as harsh, although she-wolves who were pregnant shied away from them as if Obeas could hex their unborn pups.

The time had come for Airmead to explain the dark, dirty secret of the MacHeath clan, whispered about for so many years. Airmead felt as if something deep inside herself had cracked open. And oddly enough, it felt good.

When Edme heard the Obea's name ring out, she stopped short, spreading her toes wide so she would not sink into the snow, which was piling up fast. Airmead was soon beside her.

"Follow me," Airmead said. "We'll dig a snow pit, though I think the blizzard is stopping."

Dig a snow pit — with the Obea? Edme thought. When in the history of the Beyond had a *malcadh* and an Obea ever spoken to each other? Share a snow pit with the very wolf whose task was to take *malcadhs* to their *tummfraws* to die? It was beyond astonishing to Edme. "What is it?" Edme demanded. "What do you want from me?"

"You need to hear the truth."

"I know the truth. I know what they did to me. I know that you never took me to that *tummfraw*."

"In all the time that I have been the MacHeath Obea, I have never taken any wolf pup to a *tummfraw*."

"What? Never?" Edme was astounded.

"Never!"

Almost as soon as they had settled into the snow pit, the blizzard ceased and the sun began to shine. By the time Airmead finished her story, large patches of bare ground had appeared from under the melting snow. "So you see, it's a paradox that the most depraved of all the clans has never produced an actual *malcadh*. It's as if their spirits have been deformed rather than their bodies. In a manner, that is much worse than any physical flaw." The Obea heaved a great sigh and shut her eyes tightly, as if she could not bear to say what was coming next. "When I found out I was barren, I was relieved. I didn't want to pass on the bad blood of the clan."

"But look at the MacNamara clan," said Edme. "They've produced fine wolves and they were founded by MacHeaths."

"Yes, almost a thousand years ago. The first Namara was a MacHeath wolf named Hordweard. Even to this day, some she-wolves of the MacHeath clan find their way to the MacNamara clan. The name Hordweard, of course, is cursed within our clan."

"It's not my clan anymore," Edme said stubbornly. "Anyway, I never heard the name Hordweard."

"Well, it's a forbidden word. But it's odd about things

like that; the more forbidden, the more attractive they become. Throughout the centuries, there's been a secret Hordweard Society within the MacHeath clan. Sometimes it dies out for generations, but then it reappears and a few she-wolves strong of spirit leave and seek the MacNamara clan."

By this time, their snow pit had become a puddle. "Isn't this weather odd?" said Airmead. "It was very clever of you to play on the clan's superstitions about such things. It might divert their anger for a while."

"You mean about my rejection of the clan."

"Yes. All they've ever wanted is representation at the Watch, you know."

"I didn't want to tell them who told me about my eye."

"They'll find out. They always do."

"What will they do if they find out what you told me?" Edme asked.

"It won't matter."

"Why not?"

"I'll be gone." Airmead hesitated but then continued, "I think I'm one of the last members of the Hordweard Society. And I plan to seek out the MacNamara clan. I've had it with the MacHeaths. It took me a while to get my courage up to leave, because if they find out, they'll set a *byrrgis* on me and kill me. Tear me apart."

"Were there other members before you?"

"One."

"Who was it?" Edme asked.

Airmead's eyes were such a green that they were clear, almost translucent. She looked at Edme, and her jaw began to tremble.

"Who?" Edme pressed.

"Your mother, Edme."

Edme felt a dizzying nausea swirl up within her. She shut her eyes.

Airmead continued, "Your mother's name was Akira. She left when they tore your eye out."

"Did she make it to the MacNamara clan?"

Airmead's head dropped and she shook it sadly. "She was brave, Edme. Oh, my, she was brave. That scar that runs across the chieftain's face down to his neck?"

Edme nodded.

"That was what she did to him. She was going for his eye as he had gone for yours."

CHAPTER SEVEN

TATTERS

FAOLAN GASPED. "YOUR MOTHER gave Dunbar MacHeath his scar?" Edme nodded at him. They had met up again near the marsh where they'd seen the frost-covered spiderweb. Faolan was dizzy with what Edme had told him. The false *tummfraw*. Her maiming. Her mother's courage and Edme's own courage in rejecting her clan.

"There was one more thing I forgot to tell you," Edme said.

More! Faolan thought. *What more could there be?*

"I never realized how truly superstitious the MacHeaths are. But when it started to snow, I took a chance because they were all pretty tipsy on Litha juice and I thought it might play to my advantage. I wanted them confused."

"So what did you do?"

"I commented on the strange weather for this moon. I said not since the Ice March out of the Long Cold had there been snow in this moon."

Faolan tipped his head to one side. "You did?" An odd light seemed to glimmer deep within his eyes. He rubbed his splayed paw into the ground.

"Yes. Do you think that was wrong?" Edme asked, suddenly nervous.

"No, no, not at all."

But as Edme looked at Faolan, it seemed as if he had withdrawn to some distant, unreachable place. Something within Faolan stirred like the tatters of a long-forgotten dream.

"But what will the Fengo say?" Edme asked.

"About what?" Faolan blinked. He snapped back to his old self, as if he had just taken a wander and then slipped into his own pelt once again.

"Will he reject me because I am not a true gnaw wolf?"

"But you won — you proved yourself at the *gadder-gnaw*. You are as true as any gnaw wolf, Edme."

"Perhaps he will think that accepting me will encourage others to maim pups."

"Never!" Faolan was shocked. "No clan is as savage as the MacHeaths. Don't say it. Do not even think it. Now come on; we have to get on our way."

Edme felt that she should have asked Faolan more about his *tummfraw,* but what seemed almost more important to Faolan was the return to the place where Thunderheart had first found him. Edme was sure the *drumlyn* Faolan had built to Thunderheart was beautiful, for no wolf carved bones as magnificently as Faolan did. She supposed her own mother's bones were long gone. It would have been nice, though, to make such a *drumlyn* for Akira.

Akira. She said the name softly in her head. It was a lovely sound and kept running through Edme's mind as the two wolves made their way toward the Ring of Sacred Volcanoes.

They had been traveling east, skirting the far edges of a territory in which the MacHeaths often hunted during the summer. Faolan was about to comment on how odd it was to see snow on the ground, when suddenly they came across a snow patch streaked with blood. Both wolves stopped, their hackles raised, their eyes narrowed to slits of green. A breeze caught the scent of slaughter and pushed it toward them.

Wolf blood! Edme felt a sudden chill in her marrow. *Great Lupus, let it not be her,* she prayed. Airmead's words coursed through her. *If they find out, they'll set a* byrrgis *on me and kill me. Tear me apart.*

"What has happened here?" Faolan said. It was a gruesome scene, with wolf parts scattered all over.

"Ingliss," Edme said.

"What?" Faolan asked.

"Ingliss and Kyran. I recognize their pelts." She was relieved that Airmead wasn't one of the dead wolves, but this seemed wrong, terribly wrong, even though she had loathed the sniping taunts of the young she-wolves.

"But why?"

"They are the ones who told me that I was made a *malcadh.* Dunbar MacHeath must have found out." She took a deep breath and then softly continued, "They always do. But this . . . why this? Why not the Pit?"

"The Pit?" Faolan asked. "What is the Pit?"

"Never mind," Edme replied grimly.

The two wolves gave a wide margin to the bloodied patch of snow and tried not to look at the scattered pieces of what had been silly young she-wolves whose worst crime was teasing and taunting. With each step Edme took, she felt reassured in her decision to reject her clan. At the same time, she felt she was taking a step closer toward her mother, Akira. She knew now that she came from a brave she-wolf, and this to her was as meaningful as discovering a *tummfraw*. Her journey had been exactly what the Fengo predicted — a journey toward truth, understanding, and reconciliation with her fate. Edme felt blessed to have had such a mother. *Mum*, she thought. *I found a mum!*

As Faolan and Edme walked on in silence, the snow patches appeared with less frequency. The weather evened out and started to feel as it normally did in the Moon of the Shedding Antlers, though they found fewer antlers. It was as if the migratory herds were not returning in the great numbers they usually did. The thought gave Faolan pause. Had he seen this sparseness of antlers before? There was a haunting familiarity in the scarcity. But how could this be? It was only the third summer he had ever known — only the third Moon of the Shedding Antlers he had ever experienced. Once again something rustled in Faolan, like a distant wind blowing tatters of memory from an ancient place.

He turned to Edme. "When you were in the *gadder-heal* of the MacHeaths, you mentioned the Long Cold and the Ice March and it . . . it . . ."

"Disturbed them, I think."

It disturbs me as well, Faolan thought.

They were within a day's run to the region of the Ring of Sacred Volcanoes. In spite of their excitement, they decided not to push on. They had heard that the most spectacular time to arrive at the Ring was near twilight when the volcanoes often erupted, painting the fiery swathes of flame and plumes of ash against the purpling sky. So they found a mountain cat's abandoned den and settled in for the night. There was no moon, but the stars were rising and seemed brighter than ever. An icy drizzle began to fall. Again they shook their heads in wonder at the oddities of the season. But they were too tired to speculate on the whimsies of nature and soon were fast asleep.

It was as though he were moving through a landscape that was neither earth nor sky. Deeper and deeper, Faolan traveled into a misty place where the seasons of the moons fell away. I feel as though I am wading through the shoals of time, *Faolan thought. His pelt felt loose on his shoulders, his bones insubstantial. And yet he seemed to sense a twinkling in his marrow. I am nothing and I am all.* He trotted on through the banks of rising mist. *In the distance, he spied a trail through the vapor made by a very old wolf, an "ancient," as the first wolves of the Beyond were called. The ancient was nearly toothless, and Faolan could see that his once bright green eyes had turned milky with age.* He must be almost blind, *Faolan thought, and yet the wolf looked down at the trail as if searching for something.* Hoofprints. He's looking for elk! *Faolan knew that the old wolf was bothered by the same questions Faolan had wondered over — why this scarcity of antlers? The elk had not returned.* Why? Where had they gone? *The old wolf's knees began to buckle beneath him. And it came to Faolan that the wolf had come to this remote place to begin the steps of* cleave hwlyn, *the act of separating from his clan, his pack, and finally his own body.* He is dying, *Faolan thought. His life had been fully lived, and now his time had come. Faolan watched as the stars began to break out, his marrow quivering as he saw the first rung of the star ladder that led to the Cave of Souls.* I will see him slip his pelt and climb the star ladder. Should I be watching? *Dying was a private act and yet . . . it all looked so familiar!*

But Faolan did not see the old wolf climb the star ladder. He woke up just as the last star of the night was dissolving into the gray of the dawn. He sensed he had dreamed a wonderful dream tinged with sadness, but he could remember nothing about it. Not a shred. He felt a certain peacefulness, a comfort. He looked over at Edme, who was still sleeping, and sensed that she was dreaming, too, perhaps of her mother, Akira.

PART
TWO
THE RING

CHAPTER EIGHT

VIEW FROM A RIDGE

AS FAOLAN AND EDME MADE THEIR way east toward the Ring of Sacred Volcanoes, they noticed an increasing number of owls flying up from the Hoolian kingdoms to the south. *At least,* Faolan thought, *something is moving in the right direction this moon.*

"Faolan, if we climb up this ridge, I think we might get a glimpse of the volcanoes."

"Let's go!" Faolan said. And the two wolves began to scramble up the steep slope.

When they arrived at the top of the ridge, they could see the cones of the five volcanoes in the distance. A dim rose-colored glow could be spotted over two of the volcanoes. "We're too far away to see the flames," Edme said. "But, of course, I only have one eye."

"I've got two but can't see any flames. But when we get closer at twilight, I bet we'll see them."

McLean County Unit #5
201-EJHS

"There are other ridges ahead. I can see them clearly from here," Edme yipped.

Faolan had diverted his gaze and was looking straight down. Directly below them he had spotted the river. *"Tine smyorfin,"* he whispered.

"Huh?" Edme looked at Faolan, whose eyes were trained on the river. "What's that you said? Sounds like Old Wolf."

"What are you talking about?" Faolan asked.

"That expression, *tine* something."

"I said 'by my marrow,'" Faolan answered.

"No, you didn't," Edme insisted. "You whispered something that sounded very much like Old Wolf. I may just have one eye, but I do have two ears, Faolan."

"Well, I was looking down there. See the river."

The water was no longer amber but green, green as a wolf's eyes. But what was more interesting was the scene. In a shallow part of the river, there were two wolves and a large grizzly feeding off the carcass of what appeared to be a moose. The grizzly's cubs were frolicking on the river-banks. At a short but respectful distance away, ten or so other wolves waited their turn. Periodically, the bear left to regurgitate large chunks of steaming meat for her cubs.

Faolan was mesmerized by the sight. He had heard

that on rare occasions, wolves and bears shared prey. But he'd been told it was a practice from long ago. He recalled the chieftains saying that the wolves of the Watch kept up many of the old practices.

"These have to be Watch wolves," Faolan whispered.

"Yes, I was thinking the same. I've heard they do this. It's strange, isn't it?"

Faolan did not reply. For him, it didn't seem that strange at all. He was not sure why. Partly, it was because watching these bears took him back to his youngest days as a pup, when he would wait with all the patience he could muster for Thunderheart to regurgitate the meat she had brought back from hunting. The smell of the fresh meat mingled with the juices from Thunderheart's mouth and gut rushed back to him.

"You're thinking about Thunderheart, aren't you, Faolan?" Edme asked.

"Yes." There was a small hitch in his voice. "I wish we could go down and meet these wolves."

"We can't, Faolan. The Fengo said we must go to that place, the Hot Gates, to be met and properly led into the Ring of Sacred Volcanoes."

"I wonder how we'll even know what the Hot Gates look like. Such a strange name."

"I don't know. Maybe they're little volcanoes that lead into the Ring," Edme replied. "Look, Faolan, there's an outcropping down below and downwind from the bears. We could watch the wolves from there. They'd never know."

Faolan hesitated, but the idea was irresistible. It was as if his marrow were straining to be near that mother bear and her cubs. He could catch reassuring smells on the breezes when she regurgitated meat for her cubs. Perhaps it wouldn't hurt to watch just a bit longer from a safe distance downwind.

By the time Faolan and Edme reached the outcrop, the wolves had left the moose carcass. The grizzly mom and her two cubs had stayed on the banks of the river.

"Her den must be near here. Bears like to have summer dens near a river. Good for fishing," Faolan said.

"Those cubs are so cute. Just little fur balls! Look how playful they are."

It took Faolan back. How much fun he had had with Thunderheart. He could picture himself so clearly, riding atop her shoulders or scampering after her when they hunted for roots in the early spring. How he had hated the bitter roots they dug at first. Now he would give anything to be out digging roots with his second Milk Giver.

The mother bear had a full belly and had stretched out to bask in the midday sun for a quick nap. It was odd, but Faolan himself had begun to feel sleepy. It was almost as if he had eaten all that meat and could hardly keep his eyes open to watch the cubs playing.

"I suppose, now that the wolves are gone and the mother bear seems full, we could help ourselves to what's left of the moose, couldn't we?" Edme said.

"I suppose so." Faolan yawned. "But I'm really not that hungry." He felt satiated though he had eaten nothing.

He soon fell into a dreamless sleep.

Faolan would never be quite sure what it was that awakened him or how long he had slept. But he was immediately alert. Something was not right. He laid back his ears, raised his muzzle, and slitted his eyes. *No! It can't be!* He'd resisted his own yearning to go closer to the mother grizzly — and now Edme was there playing with the cubs! Thankfully, the mother grizzly was still slumbering. If the mother bear woke up, Edme would be dead before he could warn her off. He rose up trembling. His guard hairs erect, he began walking stiff-legged as quietly as he could toward Edme and the frolicking cubs. He glanced at the mother. She was sleeping deeply. As he got closer, the cubs spotted him. He growled low at Edme.

Edme turned. There was shock in her eyes. "Faolan, whatever is the matter with you?"

"Get away from those cubs! Get away. She'll kill you if she wakes up!"

The cubs looked up, startled. Edme read the horror in Faolan's eyes and immediately backed away.

"Follow me!" he ordered and immediately began to run at press-paw speed. He looked over his shoulder. One of the cubs had tried to run after them but stopped when he realized he couldn't keep up. He had a forlorn look in his eyes. *By my marrow, he's about to cry,* Faolan thought, but he ran on.

When they had put a good distance between themselves and the grizzly, Faolan stopped. He glared at Edme.

"What is wrong with you, Faolan? You . . . you don't seem yourself at all. You really scared me!" she said.

"I'm sorry, but I was scared. If that mother grizzly woke up, we would both be dead. You can never, ever touch or even come near a grizzly's cubs like that. They go crazy, *cag mag — cag maglosc.*"

Edme blinked. Faolan was speaking Old Wolf again. And she could have sworn she'd heard him muttering strange phrases in his sleep that sounded like Old Wolf.

"I'm sorry. I didn't know," Edme said.

"You know how she-wolves are about their pups. It's a thousand times worse with grizzlies. We're used to aunties and other wolves around. But grizzlies aren't very social. They lead solitary lives."

"I'll never do it again. I promise." Edme paused. "But you have to admit they were about the cutest things ever."

"Yes, they were," he said, almost longingly. Deep within him he felt a pang — a pang of regret? A pang of loss? He wasn't sure.

CHAPTER NINE

THE HOT GATES

AS THE TWO WOLVES TRAVELED, the cones of the volcanoes became clearer and clearer, and they could see that at least three of the five volcanoes were erupting. More and more owls scored the sky. The rims of the craters loomed in the distance like ragged crowns, and from them, towering flames leaped up, raking the pale lavender of the twilight sky.

Faolan and Edme could just make out the cairns of bones on which the wolves of the Watch perched, vigilant against intruders.

"Can you believe it, Faolan?" Edme said as they drew close enough to see the wolves leaping into the air, sometimes twisting and flipping themselves about in ways they had never seen wolves move before. "Can you believe that we shall soon be there?" Edme paused. "And we're not *malcadhs* anymore! We're true gnaw wolves of the Watch!" Her voice was filled with wonder.

Faolan felt a shiver deep in his marrow. *Members.* The very word seemed to glow with a noble luster. They were to serve, no longer objects of scorn but as vital sentinels of the Watch. It was their job to guard the Ember of Hoole, the very center of this universe of wolves and owls. For the Beyond to run smoothly, the ember must be kept safe where it lay in one of the five volcanoes at the Sacred Ring.

"The volcanoes have such odd names, don't they?" Faolan said.

"H'rathghar, Kiel — I think those are owl names from the northern kingdoms," Edme replied. "H'rathghar," she repeated.

"Not H'rath . . . it's more of a growl at the back of your throat," Faolan said, correcting Edme's pronunciation. He tipped his head back and emitted a throaty *hrrr* sound.

"How do you know all this?" Edme said. When Faolan growled, the volcano's name sounded awfully authentic — not that she knew exactly what owl speech of the northern kingdoms sounded like.

Faolan shrugged. "I'm not sure." He was truly confounded and could not figure out where these wisps of knowledge came from. It was as if they were borne on a maverick river that coursed through his mind. Thunderheart had even told him that she had named him Faolan because "fao" was the word for both "wolf" and "river," and "lan" was the word for "gift." In this river that was his mind, Faolan sensed two currents — one from what he thought of as The Now and the other as The Then. The Now was easy to understand. It was The Then that perplexed him. Did all wolves have two currents in their minds?

"Let's see . . . then there are three others — Dunmore, Morgan, and Stormfast. I'm glad there are just five to learn," Edme said.

"Some of the names sound like wolf names," Faolan offered.

"Yes, Morgan does, and so does Dunmore, but I've never met a wolf named Stormfast." She paused. "Well, I guess we're about to meet a volcano called Stormfast."

A wind out of the east began to blow and both wolves stopped suddenly. Their hackles rose as they tipped their noses into the breeze.

"That's it, isn't it? The smell of the volcanoes," Faolan said.

"Not exactly pleasant. Reminds me of some rotten duck eggs I once met up with," Edme said.

"Rotten duck eggs?" Faolan repeated and then murmured, *"Tine smyorfin."*

"There, you said it again!" Edme blurted.

"Said what?"

"That Old Wolf thing you said back by the river."

"I didn't say any Old Wolf thing. I just muttered, 'by my marrow.'"

Edme tipped her head to one side and regarded her friend. *How odd,* she thought. *Faolan really doesn't know when he's saying these things. His mouth speaks in something that sounds like Old Wolf, but his ears hear it another way.*

"Well, never mind. Let's go," she replied, trotting on.

As they drew nearer to the Ring, they began to see strange rock formations that rose writhing like solid smoke. These formations were called *yondos,* and two immense ones towered above the others.

"The Hot Gates!" they both exclaimed at once.

"The Fengo said stop *at* them." The two wolves looked at each other, perplexed. A simple word such as "at" could have different interpretations. Edme, who had a very practical streak, cocked her head and regarded the two towering formations. "Well, he didn't say 'between' them, and he didn't say 'beside' them. So I would think we should just go right up to the base of one and stop there."

Just then, two howls peeled off the tops of the Hot

Gates and two wolves began to scramble down them. Faolan and Edme were transfixed. The Hot Gates were so steep, they had no idea how the wolves could make such a spectacular descent without falling to their deaths.

"Great Lupus, will you look at that!" Edme cried as the two wolves took the last twenty-five feet in two dazzling leaps. They might as well have had wings. As they landed, they appeared to bounce gently for a few feet, then began trotting toward Faolan and Edme.

They have sent wolves to greet us that are our twins! The thought streamed through both Faolan's and Edme's mind. For as the two wolves from the Watch came closer, Faolan recognized one as the wolf missing an eye whom he had seen at the *gaddergnaw* competition, and the other as the wolf with his front paw twisted backward.

Faolan and Edme sank to their knees and began the sequence of submission postures.

"Up! Up! Quickly," the flip-pawed one urged. He was a brindled wolf with swirling patches of dark brown and tawny fur. "Much to learn!"

When they rose, the she-wolf spoke. "I am Winks, and this is my fellow *taiga*, Twist."

"More properly Twistling, but Twist will do. I believe my paw speaks for my name." The brindled wolf raised his flip paw into the air and waved it about.

Winks now continued, "We don't indulge in excessive formality here. It takes up too much time and there's so much for you to learn."

"But don't let that fool you," Twist said. "If you thought your life was tough as gnaw wolves, it will be tougher now."

"Don't frighten them, Twist," Winks said.

"I don't think these young'uns are easily frightened, Winks." He turned to Faolan and Edme. "Follow us and we'll escort you to the Ring."

The ring of volcanoes was smaller in circumference than Faolan and Edme had expected, although at press-paw speed, it would take almost half a day to complete the circle. They entered through the Dunmore-H'rathghar quadrant, named for the two volcanoes that dominated this section of the Ring. Between the two volcanoes were four large *drumlyns* of gnawed bones that rose to an impressive height. Atop each one, a gnaw wolf was perched, now and then shooting high into the air to perform jumps as spectacular as those they had witnessed from Twist and Winks. Faolan was known for his impressive leaps, which he had learned while attempting to walk on his hind legs like Thunderheart. These wolves, however, executed fantastic somersaults, twists, and turns in the air. Were they just showing off or was there some purpose to their staggering feats of agility? No sooner did the question come to Faolan's mind than Twist answered it.

"I imagine you're wondering about the aerial tumbling you see. The wolves are not showing off — although that's not beyond them. They're monitoring the plumes of ash and observing the cool glow of the embers."

"Cool glow?" Edme said.

"It's a term, one of many that you shall learn, that helps us understand the behavior of the volcanoes, their stages of eruption and so forth," Winks replied. "Come along now."

"It's the new gnaw wolves!" one wolf cried out midair as he swung into a high arc, then tucked his hind legs in tightly and came down in a loop. "Welcome to the Ring!" he cried. A chorus of hullos rang out.

It was all so different from what Faolan and Edme had expected. In the Beyond, the wolves of the Watch were thought of as austere in their ways, aloof and not at all social with those outside their clans. But Edme and Faolan were being welcomed with great enthusiasm and in the most cheerful manner.

CHAPTER TEN

THE BONE OF BONES

AS THE TWO YOUNG WOLVES entered the *gadderheal* of the Watch, the Fengo rose from a bed of pelts to greet them.

"Welcome to the Ring," Finbar the Fengo said. "We wolves of the Watch serve as the highest governing wolf body in the Beyond. We decide territorial boundaries, settle clan disputes, and are the Supreme *Raghnaid*, the final court for amending and creating new laws. But our most important task is to guard the Ember of Hoole, which lies buried in one of the five volcanoes. If this powerful ember comes into the talons of a graymalkin owl, there is mortal danger for all species, from the wolves, owls, and caribou, down to the smallest rodent."

The Fengo's green eyes slitted as he looked at the two young wolves. "Now the time has come for you to think in a new way. You must learn to think like a wolf of the Watch."

Edme shifted nervously on her feet and looked down. *But am I truly a wolf of the Watch if I was not born a mal-cadh?* She had felt so brave when she told the MacHeaths she would join the Watch as a free runner. Now she was too frightened to say anything.

The Fengo continued, "In protecting the ember from your posts on the *drumlyns*, it is important to realize that it's not how high you jump that matters, but what you learn when you are jumping. What you see. What you feel. What you smell. Our focus is the five volcanoes. You shall learn their natural history — their temperaments." He took a step closer to the two wolves. "We exist in a close relationship with the owls of Ga'Hoole. The connection goes back to the very beginnings of our time here in the Beyond. When the good King Hoole first discovered the ember, he made a pact with the wolves that we guard it until an appointed king appeared to retrieve it." He paused again. "There is much to learn, is there not?"

Faolan and Edme both nodded.

"Our late Fengo, Hamish, has set much of our history down on the Bone of Bones. I now present you with it." He turned to another Watch wolf, a silver wolf with no ears who brought out the bone tucked under her chin and dropped it at their feet.

"Here, young'uns," she said softly. The bone gleamed with Hamish's careful incising, exquisitely elegant yet bold.

"B-b-but . . . b-but," Edme stammered. "How do we know a graymalkin? Does it tell on the Bone of Bones?"

The Fengo and the silver wolf, who was named Colleen, both shook their heads. "There is much you can learn from the Bone of Bones, but mostly you'll learn through experience," the Fengo said. "The Bone does not tell you how to recognize a graymalkin. It is an instinct that you will develop, a sense that an owl is not merely looking for coals. Graymalkins spend a lot of their time flying low around the edges of the craters, making false passes over the ember beds that spill down the slopes."

"But how can you tell the difference between a false pass and a true one?" Faolan asked.

"Your *taigas* will school you in this. They are your greatest resource." He nodded at Twist and Winks.

But do I deserve a taiga? thought Edme. *How will they treat me if they know the truth? I have to tell them. I have to!*

The Fengo continued, "Twist and Winks here are ready to answer your questions. You shall begin your service at the cairns of their present assignments. You will be shown to your den now. A busy time is coming. Do you have any questions?"

Edme gave Faolan a nervous glance. He nodded just slightly. She knew that the time had come for her to tell the Fengo the truth — how she was not a true *malcadh* but was made one by the depravity of the MacHeath clan. She took a step forward, holding her head high and squinting with her single eye so she could better keep the Fengo in focus. She did not want to appear to be cowering in fear or shame. She would be honest and dignified as she told the horrible truth.

"Honorable Fengo, I learned much on my *Slaan Leat*. As you told us when we set out, it was a journey toward truth. In the course of my journey, I discovered a terrible secret."

The Fengo cocked his head; his eyes remained unblinking. Edme felt their penetrating gaze. "Go on," he said. A new severity had crept into his voice.

"I am not a true *malcadh*."

There was a sharp inhalation of breath. "What are you saying?" the Fengo asked.

"I was born normal and then was disfigured. My eye was torn out." She wanted to tell the Fengo so much more. She wanted to tell him that the scar Dunbar MacHeath bore, that ragged line raking across his face, was caused by her mother, Akira. She wanted to tell him about Ingliss and Kyran. But she knew she must get to the point. "I come here not as a representative of the MacHeath clan, but as a free runner. I represent no one except myself." Edme looked down at her front paws. She could not bear to meet the Fengo's eyes.

"Look at me, Edme," he said sharply. And when she finally looked up, she did not see anger on Finbar's face, only sadness. "It was the MacHeaths who did this to you?"

"It was Dunbar," Edme answered.

The Fengo sighed deeply before speaking. "There have been rumors of this in the past. Now you have confirmed our worst suspicions. These MacHeaths are not true clan wolves. They deserve no place in the Beyond. As Fengo of the Watch, I invoke the privilege accorded only to myself as chieftain of the Supreme *Raghnaid* to call together a Court of *Crait*."

There was a gasp from the wolves. Never in living memory had such a court been called. If the MacHeaths were judged *crait*, the entire clan would be cast out of the Beyond. From that moment, they would be outclanners.

It felt as if all the air had suddenly been sucked out of the den. Edme staggered slightly, then dropped her tail, tucked it flat between her legs, and began to turn away.

"Where are you going?" the Fengo asked. But she hardly heard him. "Edme, halt! I asked, where are you going?"

She stopped and turned. An immense tear began to shimmer in her single eye. "The clan I came from is to be judged. I'm not welcome here."

"What absolute nonsense, my dear," the Fengo said.

Then another wolf stepped forward. She was a red wolf also missing one eye. Edme had seen her at the *gaddergnaw* and then again as they entered the Fengo's den.

"Pardon me, honorable Fengo."

"Yes, Banja. You have something to say?"

"I only want to suggest that we not be hasty in our decisions. By her own confession, Edme is a *malcadh* made. So perhaps it is not quite appropriate that . . . that . . ."

"That what?" The Fengo's voice had taken on a frightening edge.

"That she serve in the same capacity as the rest of us. Perhaps it would be advisable that she continue in her gnaw wolf status for a while, at least."

The Fengo stalked forward on stiff legs, his tail high,

his teeth bared. "Banja, you have become as prickly as a burr. There is no purpose to be served in this youngster continuing as a gnaw wolf. She must train to become a wolf of the Watch. Do I have to invoke the privilege of the Sayer to discipline a Watch wolf? I have never used it before — please do not tempt me now!"

Faolan and Edme watched as Banja seemed to shrink in her own pelt. She backed away, her single eye that only a second before glittered now seemed dull as a dry stone.

The Fengo turned his back to Banja, who was slinking into the shadows at the rear of the *gadderheal*. "Edme, you are not *crait*. You did not do this to yourself. It was the clan, led by its chieftain, that did this to you. By calling them for a Court of *Crait*, we ensure that they will never again maim a wolf to make a *malcadh*. If they are found guilty, they will have no say in any councils held in the *gadderheals* of the Beyond. Let them destroy themselves. But you, Edme, represent no one except yourself. You have an amazing ability to carve bones. You performed beyond expectation in the *byrrgis* at the *gaddergnaw* when you plunged in for the kill rush." He glanced briefly at Faolan, who cringed at the memory of his lapse of attention at that crucial moment.

Edme, he thought, *deserves to serve in the Watch more than I. She made no mistakes during the entire competition.* Faolan had simply excelled in carving, which seemed to have made up for his errors on the *byrrgis.*

"So I say to you, Edme, you are a true Watch wolf despite the deceit of the MacHeath clan. You are a loyal wolf despite their faithless desecration of our most sacred laws. You shall serve with honor and dignity despite having been raised in a clan marked by dishonor and disgrace. We welcome you as a free runner." Edme felt her marrow trembling. The huge tear that had welled in her eye now ran down her face.

The Fengo paused and looked at Faolan. "We welcome you as a free runner, Edme, and you, Faolan, as the best of your clan. Now Twist and Winks will lead you to your den. At the first phase of the newing, your training will begin."

"Newing?" Edme whispered as they followed Twist and Winks. "What's that?"

"It's an owl word for the new moon. They call it *dwenking* when it begins to fade," Faolan replied.

"Where did you learn so much Hoolian?" Edme asked.

"From Gwynneth — she's a Rogue smith." Rogue smiths were owls who worked metal but lived apart from other owls.

Twist overheard them. "Ah! Gwynneth. She'll be coming soon. It is getting to be the season of Morgan and Stormfast. The Rogue smiths particularly love the embers from these two volcanoes. And when the She-Winds blow, both volcanoes begin their most violent eruptions at the same time. It seems like every Rogue smith and Rogue collier throughout the Hoolian kingdoms descends upon us. Oh, what a time it is! But now here is your den. Your training begins shortly, so get some rest."

"Look at this," Faolan marveled as they slid down a steep passage into the den. "They've even given us pelts. I've never slept on a pelt of my own. I only got the discarded ones from my pack after pups had wet them so often they stank."

"Me never!" Edme said. "Even ones soiled by pups were too good for me."

They each circled their pelts three times as was the custom with most wolves before settling down for a sleep. The pelts were caribou — winter caribou, so they were all the thicker.

"Edme," Faolan said. "I think I'm too excited to sleep."

"Me, too, but we should try."

"Yes, let's try," Faolan replied.

They were silent for a while. Then Faolan piped up again. "Edme, are you asleep yet?" He waited. "Edme? Are you sleeping?"

"Well, I was until you asked me." She yawned.

"Oh, sorry."

"It's all right," Edme replied. "What is it?"

"I think what you did back there in the Fengo's den, what you said — you know, the truth about yourself. It was very brave of you."

"Thank you, Faolan." *You woke me up to tell me I was brave?*

They both nestled deeper into their caribou pelts.

"They smell so good, don't they? No pup pee," Faolan said.

"Yep, no pup pee."

Just as Edme was drifting off once again, Faolan said, "You're not asleep yet, are you, Edme?"

"Almost," she huffed.

"I just want to say one more thing."

"Yes, what's that?"

"You really do deserve to be here — much more than I do. I mean, you made the kill rush."

Edme's hackles raised. "Faolan, that is just plain

stupid. I have never heard anything more *cag mag* in my life. You have proven yourself time and time again. Now, kindly let me sleep."

But still he could not sleep. So he turned to the Bone of Bones. It was not easy to read in the darkness of the cave, but he soon found that certain sections had been carved deeper, and if he ran his tongue over them he could feel the inscription. One section in particular had been carved very deeply as if for extra emphasis. His marrow trembled as he began to read a passage.

There has been a bond between the wolves and the grizzlies in the region of the sacred volcanoes that is vitally important. It is the reason why two species of animals — the top meat eaters of the region — can live peacefully together. Nowhere else in the Beyond do wolves and bears live in such close harmony. But let it be known that there are certain customs that are practiced between ourselves and the bears of the Beyond to ensure that we will always live harmoniously with one another in this small realm within the larger one of the Beyond. One of the most important rules of behavior is that a wolf must never touch the cub of a grizzly, for there is no telling what bloody havoc might ensue, the least of which would be the death of that single wolf.

There are other practices followed that also ensure that the grizzlies and the wolves of the Watch will continue. Good relations between ourselves and the bears is essential because our range for hunting is limited; therefore we must live together peaceably.

"*Urskadamus,*" Faolan muttered the bear curse he had heard Thunderheart use was she was deeply irritated. His curse had awakened Edme.

"What are you doing?"

"Reading the Bone of Bones."

"In this light?"

"The bone is carved deeply. I can feel it with my tongue." There was utter anguish in Faolan's voice.

"Faolan, what is it?"

He looked up at Edme. *Does she know how close she came to being killed?*

"Did you touch the cub?" Faolan whispered.

"I don't think so." Her voice was taut with fear.

CHAPTER ELEVEN

DUNBAR MACHEATH CONSIDERS

"I FOLLOWED THEM FOR A DAY and a night, until they came to rest on a cliff just above the river. There was a moose carcass on the sandbar in the shallow part of the river. A grizzly and a *byrrgis* from the Watch were sharing the kill."

"What!" The wolves who had gathered in the MacHeath *gadderheal* gasped. There was a flurry of exclamations.

"Shut up!" the chieftain ordered. "They do that sort of thing — the wolves of the Watch and the bears have a close bond. Go on, Fretta, this is getting interesting, very interesting!"

"The grizzly's cubs were on the banks and she was bringing the meat back to them. When they had all had their fill and the wolves had left, the mother bear napped. The cubs were not a bit tired."

"Of course, the mother did all the work." Katria, a she-wolf with a pelt black as a moonless night, spoke softly. But not softly enough. The chieftain leaped upon her and sank his fangs into her haunch. Blood spritzed out of his muzzle from a small cut made by the Litha thorns, which made him even angrier. So he swatted Katria and she skidded across the floor of the *gadderheal*. "No more from you!" Katria slunk off to a corner. Lying as flat as she could, with her muzzle buried in her paws, she wished herself invisible. How much more could she take of this clan? Kyran had been her daughter — her foolish, foolish daughter. Katria's mate had not even been that disturbed when Dunbar MacHeath dispatched the *slink melf* to kill Kyran and Ingliss. All that mattered to her mate, Donaidh, was rising in the ranks of the lords.

In Old Wolf, the word *donaidh* meant "ruler of the world," and Katria's mate seemed to feel that this alone gave him the right to succeed the chieftain Dunbar, who was growing older and meaner by the day.

Katria returned her attention to the scout's report on the wolves and the bears.

"Edme and Faolan had been watching from on top of a bluff. It was the hot, lazy time of the day and soon Faolan was sleeping soundly. But not Edme. She got up and went over to play with the cubs, until Faolan awakened, darted out, and shooed her away."

The chieftain chuckled. "If the bear had awakened, she would have made short work of the two."

"Too bad," Blyden said.

"No, not at all," Dunbar countered. "I want more out of this than the death of a stupid little she-wolf like Edme. There is more to be gained than you might suspect."

"He's a wily one, our chief," someone murmured.

"There is one more thing, sir," Fretta said.

"And what is that?"

Fretta appeared suddenly very nervous. She shifted her eyes away from the chieftain and took a step backward. "There is a rumor . . . just a rumor, mind you."

"What kind of a rumor?" Dunbar MacHeath's voice dropped.

"I heard some owls discussing it, but the rumor is that the Fengo is calling our clan to the Supreme *Raghnaid* for a Court of *Crait*."

"A Court of *Crait*!" Dunbar MacHeath shot into the air so high he scraped the stone ceiling of the *gadderheal* cave. A wailing rose from the assembled wolves.

"Silence," he roared. An immediate hush fell upon the *gadderheal*. Dunbar MacHeath began to pace up and down the length of the cavern. He stopped and rolled his eyes up toward the ceiling, then regained his composure. "*Crait*, they say! *Crait!* Well, we'll show them who's *crait* and who isn't.

"The little she-wolf lassie has a fondness for grizzly cubs, eh?" he spoke reflectively. "That could get her into a lot of trouble if it were to be found out. For too long, the clans of the Beyond have been beholden to the Watch. And now they call a Court of *Crait* to judge us! This is nonsense. It is time to restore honor and power to the clans and their chieftains."

This, thought Katria, *has nothing to do with honor and everything to do with power. Raw power.*

Dunbar MacHeath regarded the wolves around him. "What is honor? Honor is doing the right thing. For years now, the wolves at the Watch have determined our clan territories, our hunting grounds. It was the wolves of the Watch and the first Fengo who decided this. Why are we a Fengo-centered land? The center of the Beyond is not the Ring, but Great Lupus! We shall ask what would Lupus do to restore our honor. We have been shackled to the Ring of Sacred Volcanoes for too long. Our duty is to restore honor!"

There were loud growls and barks of approval until

the chieftain snapped the command for quiet. A thick silence settled upon the gathered wolves as their cunning chieftain spun his net of promises. "This wolf Edme could have offered us a chance for power at the Ring, but she betrayed us. Your first thought is 'Let the grizzly mother take her retribution on the faithless Edme.' But what does one wolf killed by a grizzly amount to? Not much. Instead, we'll use this idiot wolf's behavior to spark a war that will restore our honor."

Oh, so that is what Lupus would do? Katria thought. *Start a war?*

"What kind of a war?" Blyden asked.

Dunbar MacHeath's paw flashed out and slammed Blyden sideways. "Do not interrupt! I am speaking of a war between the wolves of the Watch and the bears. There are many bears in the valley near the Sacred Ring. If they rose up, it would be the end of the Watch as we know it."

"And then what?" the chieftain's mate asked.

"And then, finally, it will be our turn."

"Our turn!" There was a low murmuring of agreement, which began to swell among the wolves. "Our turn! Our turn!" The words flowed through the *gadderheal* like a chant.

Resentment festered like a canker within the MacHeaths, carefully cultivated and nurtured by their twisted minds.

"So what is your" — It was Malan, the second-highest-ranking wolf next to the chieftain. He hesitated slightly before completing his thought — "your design, Lord Chieftain?"

"Simply this: We need a hostage. I think the cub — the cub Edme played with."

"And where will we keep this hostage?" Malan asked.

"The Pit with Old Cags," Dunbar said with a low snarl.

Katria's blood froze. Did this chieftain's depravity know no bounds?

"Aaaah!" The exclamation rippled through the *gadderheal*.

"Yes, your old chieftain still has a few tricks up his ruff." Dunbar's hackles stood up rigidly, and he gave a quick venomous glance at Donaidh.

The Pit was patrolled by Old Cags, a MacHeath wolf with the foaming-mouth disease. When a young pup was disobedient, the most effective threat was "I'll send you to Old Cags in the Pit. He'll learn you a thing or two — if you survive." Very few pups ever died in the Pit. Old Cags had barely a tooth left in his head to bite with. It was just that when a pup returned, it was changed. Pups came back in a perpetual daze, frozen into permanent postures of submission. They did not have the foaming-mouth disease, but it was as if they were in a state of brain fever and they tended to die young. Katria's mind swirled, and her gut wrenched with revulsion at the idea of condemning an innocent cub to hellfire on earth, a dim world created by her own despicable clan.

A wave of nausea washed over Katria. This would indeed spark a war between the bears and the wolves and even the owls. Total chaos! It was precisely what the MacHeaths wanted, for if they were to be declared *crait*, they were determined to bring the entire Beyond down with them.

CHAPTER TWELVE

First Watch

"HURRY ALONG NOW. NO TIME to waste! You can't be late for your first night of training." Twist and Winks had scrambled down the steep sloping entrance of the den.

"I don't suppose you've slept a wink, or should I say a Winks?" The brown wolf squinted with her good eye.

"Probably not," Twist said. "I remember how excited I was on my first night here. But you don't want to be late. Snowdon gets incredibly cranky if he has to stay on even a second beyond his shift, and Colleen, too."

"Colleen? Snowdon? Are they our *taigas*, too?"

"Oh, no, dear," Winks replied. "We are your *taigas*. They are just the Watch wolves for Morgan and Stormfast this cycle. The moon claw will be up soon."

"Moon claw?" Faolan asked.

"That's the first phase of the newing," Edme said quickly. "Because it looks like a wolf's claw."

"Yes, indeed," Winks replied. "You must have been studying the Bone of Bones."

Faolan and Edme followed their two *taigas* out of the den and began trotting at a brisk pace toward the easternmost side of the Ring. It was a strange and wondrous landscape. There was a brittle crunching sound beneath their feet as they crossed the rivers of lava that had flowed down the slopes and solidified into sheets of black glass. Flames licked the night like tongues of fire. The wolves on watch seemed determined to touch the sky as they sprang into the air to look for graymalkins.

The volcanoes were becoming slightly more active. The moonless night was scored by the tracery of red sparks. High arcing streams of embers mingled with the ice-bright stars in an astral dance through the darkness. And in the background came the wild music of the Watch wolves baying. Never had Faolan and Edme heard such howling. Each cry, each voice enlarged by the other, gaining a deep resonance. It was as if Faolan's and Edme's ears were being opened to a new universe of sound. Oddly enough, the howling was not nearly as loud as what they'd heard living with their packs. It was of a lower volume but a more powerful intensity, as if these Watch wolves had discovered a voice composed only of the strongest chords.

Both Edme and Faolan felt their throats open up. They longed to howl and yet felt it would not be right. As if reading their minds, Twist turned to them. "Your turn to howl will come when you mount the cairns. I know it's almost irresistible."

"But will we ever howl as beautifully?" Edme asked.

"You will," Winks said softly. "It takes time, but you will. The music seeps into you and settles in your marrow."

"Well, it's about time!" Snowdon, an ash-colored wolf, leaped down from the cairn that rose directly in front of Stormfast. At first, Snowdon appeared to be an ordinary wolf with no obvious deformity. All of his legs were straight, no paws were turned, he wasn't missing his eyes, ears, or tail. Faolan and Edme couldn't conceal their curiosity that this perfectly formed wolf was a member of the Watch. "Can't figure it out, can you?" Snowdon barked in a harsh voice quite different from his howling. Then he stuck his tongue out. Edme and Faolan both jumped back. It was forked, like a snake's. Snowdon laughed.

"He's all about shock," Winks muttered. "Loves shocking newcomers."

"Snowdon's going back to his den, and do you know the first thing he'll do before he sleeps?" Twist said.

"What?" asked Faolan.

"He will gnaw a log to record what he observed on his watch — any owls coming for coals, any possible gray-malkins. And he will also report on the activity of the volcano. But up you go now, Faolan. This is your cairn, and your watch is Stormfast. Winks will lead Edme to the cairn for Morgan. Scramble up, and I will join you shortly."

There was much to learn that first night.

"I am your *taiga*," Twistling said, "but so is Stormfast." He nodded toward the volcano, whose crater was belching great rolling plumes of steam that unfurled and stretched across the night. "You'll learn how the scent of the sulfurous steams varies through the seasons.

"Lava flows are rare," Twist continued, "but you will learn the difference between flows from Stormfast or from Kiel on the opposite side of the Ring."

In the eastern sky, the first bright shadow of the moon clawed its way over the horizon and began to climb. It was then that Faolan spotted the owls. Their broad wings printed against the dark, their tip feathers silvered by the moon's light, the owls of Ga'Hoole came silently through the night — ghostly and majestic.

"They usually arrive when the moon is rising. And from the cairns of Stormfast and Morgan, you have the best view of them. On the Bone of Bones, you will learn about the truly great owls, beginning with the first more than a thousand years ago." Faolan felt something in his marrow. His eyes widened and he shoved his ears forward. He, as all wolves in the Beyond, knew of the ember that lay buried in the volcanoes and how it often traveled through the lava tunnels from one crater to another. He had been told the legends of the Ring and was aware that the first King Hoole had known about the ember's strange power before he retrieved it. The King named it the Ember of Hoole and warned the first collier that this ember was not for any Rogue smith's fires.

"I know," Faolan said quietly.

"You know." Twist cocked his head and looked at Faolan with curiosity. "You've already read that part of the Bone."

"No. Not yet."

"Then how do you know?"

Faolan looked at Twist. There was confusion in his eyes. "I'm not sure. I just know."

Something stirred in Twist. It wasn't a feeling so much in his marrow as in his heart. He continued, "As I said, you'll learn about the Fengos as well as the great colliers — like Grank, the first collier."

Faolan gave a start as he heard the name.

"Are you all right?" Twist asked.

"I'm fine. Please go on." When Twist had said that name — Grank — there was a shiver deep in Faolan's marrow. The kind of shiver that wolves felt when another wolf walked over the place where they would take their last breath.

"Let's begin with the scanning leaps."

"Scanning leaps?"

To answer the question, Twist shot up as fast as any burning ember and spun around at the highest point of his leap. He did a forward somersault and landed neatly back on the cairn. Faolan blinked in astonishment.

"That was a full gainer with a double spiral and a little something of my own devising at the end. But the real point is not how fancy you can get but how much you can see while you're up there. How much you can scan in the shortest amount of time. We can't fly like owls, but . . ." Twist chuckled a bit. "Well, we try!

"Right now, your job is to learn about the good owls, not the graymalkins yet — how to recognize them, who they are.

"And now," Twist said. "Time for your first jump. The trick is to spring from your back legs and immediately tuck your front legs under. Don't try anything fancy on this first one. Just up and down and land on your hind legs."

On the count of three, Faolan sprang. Burning embers whizzed by him and he could feel the heat of the flames from the volcano and smell the lava thick and boiling in the crater. Hot gusts brushed his pelt, and for a few seconds, he felt as if he were one with the sky — the stars, the moon, the racing clouds — until he saw an owl high above him. *What a world they live in!* he thought. Before he knew it, he was back on top of the cairn.

"Your jump was very high and that is good. But for now, I would sacrifice a bit of height so you can better master the flips and twists."

Meanwhile, atop the cairn on Morgan, Edme was also concentrating hard on her jumps. She did not attain the height she desired, but her form was good, even excellent, until she caught sight of Banja below, sneering at her. She came down hard on her rump.

"Ouch!"

"Ah, you were distracted!" Winks said. "Can't let that happen. What pulled your attention away?"

Edme was reluctant to say that it was Banja. She didn't want to sound as if she were complaining, blaming someone else for her mistakes. But inside her head, she was cursing the wolf who had lodged like a burr inside her brain ever since the meeting with the Fengo. *I am not going to let her do this to me,* Edme silently vowed. *She wants to get at me and she won't!*

Edme squared up for her next jump. She took off beautifully, tucked her legs just as instructed to reduce the wind, soared as high as she had yet, then rounded down for what would have been a perfect landing, until a loud cackling burst out below her. Once more, she landed on her rump.

"Hey, quiet down there!" Winks shouted.

"Oh, we didn't realize we were so loud," Banja said. "Sorry, Winks. I was just telling Paddy that joke you told me the other night about the caribou who tried to play *biliboo.*"

"First of all, it was a limerick, not a joke. And

secondly, with the wind in this direction, your words carry and I am trying to do some serious instruction up here."

"Yes, I see she does need it. So sorry. My apologies to both of you," Banja answered. Winks looked at Edme, a perplexed expression shining in the *taiga's* single eye.

"Hmmm" was all she said.

Did that apology sound as phony to Winks as it did to me? Edme wondered.

Back atop Stormfast, Faolan worked hard on his jumps until the very end of the watch. Twist led him on a much longer trail back to the den so Faolan could see the changing of the Watch shifts at the other volcanoes.

"We're coming up on Kiel now. That's Leitha just going up to the cairn."

Faolan saw a black wolf with a glossy pelt and three legs nimbly make her way up the cairn. When she reached the top, she sprang into the air, executing a dazzling backward somersault. Faolan gasped. "She did that on only three legs!"

"Yes, indeed," Twist replied. "Some think that Leitha is the best jumper of the Watch."

Faolan could not help being ashamed that he'd once felt so special because of his jumps.

They had almost completed the circle and were approaching the volcano Dunmore when Twist stopped. Directly ahead was a cairn, but no wolf stood atop it. It was not as tall as the other cairns, but as Faolan looked at it, he felt a shudder pass through him. His hackles rose.

"The cairn of the Fengos," Twist said quietly. "This is where their bones rest and many of the bones they carved. When their time is near, when *cleave hwlyn* is approaching, they begin to carve their final bone, their Bone of Passage. It's their last thoughts before they leave this world and begin their climb up the star ladder to the Cave of Souls. That bone is buried with them deep in the cairn. The Fengos carve in a code understood only by them."

Faolan cocked his head to one side and stared at the cairn. The voice of Twist ebbed away, the baying of the wolves faded as well, and it was as if he had been transported to a moment outside of time. He felt as though he were standing next to his own pelt, looking at himself. *I know the code.*

"Faolan! Are you all right?" Twist asked.

Instantly, Faolan was back in his own skin. "Fine, good!" And he did feel good, as if he'd had a long, restful sleep.

"Look, Dunmore is awakening." The two wolves turned their heads toward the volcano, which had suddenly begun to spew geysers of hot coals into the black folds of the night. The sky was spangled with burning embers. For the first time since Thunderheart had died, Faolan felt at peace, content. *I am happy*, Faolan thought. *I am truly happy.*

CHAPTER THIRTEEN

ESCAPE OF
THE SHE-WOLVES

KATRIA'S DEN SEEMED SO TERRI-
bly empty since Kyran had been killed. She had been a
silly little wolf, but Katria could not believe her daughter
meant any real harm. It was very tempting to blame
Ingliss, her best friend, for Kyran's character flaws. Ingliss
had always dominated Kyran. But that wasn't fair either.
Ingliss's mother, Pegeen, had been killed the year before in
a mating dispute. Such disputes were not uncommon in the
MacHeath clan. Some lord of higher rank took a fancy to
a she-wolf and normally had to fight it out with the she-
wolf's mate. But this time, Ingliss's mother had stepped
into the fray to object and called the lord a stupid cur.
Well, that was the end of her. Malan, the pursuing male,
forgot Pegeen's beauty and lashed out at her, ripping open
her neck. As she was dying, Pegeen managed to bite him
and draw blood.

It was from Pegeen that Ingliss got her spirit. Now, Katria thought Pegeen was lucky to have escaped the horror of knowing that her only daughter had been murdered. What kind of life was this?

Katria's mate, Donaidh, entered the den. "Well, you made a spectacle of yourself at the *gadderheal*," he snarled. Katria didn't answer him. "Oh, you're getting all sulky on me, are you?"

He advanced on her to give her a bite. After all, he had to keep up with his chieftain, who had drawn her blood back there in the *gadderheal*. But this time, Katria did not cower; she did not sink to her knees and commence the submission postures as she normally did. She stood up, shoved her ears forward, peeled her lips back, and growled. Donaidh was stunned.

"What are you doing?" he snarled.

Katria did not answer but took a step forward and continued growling.

"Well, let me tell you something! I'm going with the chieftain and Malan and Blyden and Fretta. Yes, you idiot she-wolf. I'm going after the cub and then you'll see. I'll be promoted. I might rise nearly as high as Malan."

It was obvious to Katria that Donaidh had not seen the malicious look that Dunbar MacHeath had shot him in the *gadderheal*. Katria knew Donaidh was aiming to succeed Dunbar, but he was *not* Dunbar's choice. She sensed that Donaidh might be walking right into one of Dunbar's tricks. He had never before been invited to join a *slink melf* or any other special mission. They needed him for all the wrong reasons.

But Donaidh was musing now about his luck at being selected for this cubnapping mission. "We'll see who is dominant in this den. Remember, Dunbar has no sons to succeed him as chieftain of the clan. His mate is too old. But I am not old, nor are you. You could be the mate of the next chieftain, the mother of one someday."

Never, Katria thought. *I shall never bring another pup into this clan.* But she cast her eyes down in a semblance of submission. "We'll see," she replied in a docile voice.

"I thought you would."

Donaidh turned and ran out of the den to join Dunbar, Malan, Blyden, and the scout Fretta, who had tracked Edme to the river where she had played with the bear cubs.

As Katria watched Donaidh vanish from the entrance of the den, she knew the time had come. She must leave the MacHeath clan for good and seek refuge with the MacNamaras. She-wolves had tried in the past, but they rarely succeeded — at least not in Katria's lifetime. But now the chieftain, his highest lieutenant, her own mate, and two of the best scouts were heading out of the MacHeath territory to look for a bear cub. The time to go was now!

She would leave in broad daylight as if she were going to hunt for small prey — rodents or marmots. Her trail would take her north and east, toward a peninsula jutting out into the Hoolemere Sea.

Over the centuries, a secret language had evolved among the abused females of the MacHeath clan. In Old Wolf, this language was called *banuil caint*, which roughly translated to "she-wolf talk." There had been whispers about it for centuries. But it remained a mystery how the abused females learned *banuil caint*. The language was said to have been invented by Hordweard, the founder of the MacNamara clan. Hordweard had lived a thousand years before, in the time of the first embered monarch, King Hoole. When she escaped the MacHeath clan, her mate, the chieftain Dunleavy MacHeath, had tried to follow her. Near Broken Talon Point, she had slain him.

Hordweard went on to form her own clan and became known as Namara, which in the Old Wolf language meant "maker of strong spirits." It was said that ever since the clan was founded, secret agents of the MacNamaras left bones with Hordweard's hidden language gnawed into them in MacHeath territory, to embolden the she-wolves who wanted to flee.

Katria had found a *banuil caint* bone shortly after she gave birth to her first litter. She didn't really understand it but somehow sensed that this bone was meant for her. It took her years to decipher it, and when she did, it ignited a small glow deep within her marrow. The words were simple. *You are good. You are wise.* She had deciphered the bone after Donaidh lashed out at her, calling her a mangy cur and ripping off her dewclaw, the fifth claw on one of her front paws. There had been other messages since. None of them were addressed specifically to Katria — they could have been meant for any she-wolf who had suffered a harsh life in the Beyond's most brutal clan — but Katria seemed to find them at moments of utter darkness and despair. The most recent she found soon after the death of Kyran. She buried the bones where no one would discover them.

Through the years, the language had become easier and easier for her to comprehend. The messages were never demanding or didactic. They never told her what to do or even suggested a course of action, for the words did not seek to teach as much as to make her believe in herself and her own power. Most important, the bones of the *banuil caint* allowed her to reflect deeply on her life and its meaning. Gradually, she began to believe in her own worth. With this belief came a trust in her dignity as a living creature on earth. It became clear to her that nothing was owed her but that there were things she needed to do if she wanted to live a life of courage instead of fear.

And now the MacHeaths were planning a war, and Katria knew she had to leave. If anyone could stop the war, it would not be the wise wolves of the Watch but the MacNamara clan. For no one knew the ways of the MacHeaths better than the MacNamaras. And no wolf was braver than a MacNamara she-wolf. They were slow to anger, but once set upon, a spark ignited deep within them that forged their marrow into stone. It was as if flint ran in their bones.

@

Katria set off shortly before dawn, just after the departure of her chief and his top lieutenants to grab a cub. Katria blessed the prevailing wind that would speed her journey and slow the chieftain on his own diabolical mission in the opposite direction. Her journey would take longer, but she planned to travel at press-paw speed. Females were the strongest runners in any wolf pack, and outflankers were the strongest of all. She felt a kindling in her bones. Was it the flint of the MacNamaras? She was determined to get to them in time.

She had been on the trail for a while but was not in the least tired. The words of the *banuil caint* seemed to sing down her bones, and with each step, she became increasingly invigorated. As high noon approached and her shadow grew shorter, a bright shadow inside her seemed to be growing. Katria did not have a name for it. She had never before felt this sense of emboldened spirit expanding within her.

A sound emanated from a sparse copse of birches and brambly thornbushes, and Katria stopped for a moment. She knew in her marrow that if Donaidh followed her, she would slay him. Something white moved in the thicket. Her hackles rose. Was it a *slink melf*?

She crouched into a defensive posture but shoved her ears forward. The days of submission to tyrants were over. Like a silent rebellion, the words of the *banuil caint* rumbled through her marrow.

But it was not a tyrant who stepped into the clearing. It was Airmead the Obea. It was as if she had materialized from the very bark of the birches.

"You!" Katria gasped.

"Yes. You were not the only one reading those bones. But you were much braver. I left when I knew you would."

"But how did you know? Were you the only one who saw me leave?"

"I didn't see you leave. I saw when you decided to go."

"B-b-but . . . b-but . . ." Katria stammered. "You weren't in the den when Donaidh and I argued."

"I was in the *gadderheal* when the chieftain lashed out at you. I saw your eyes as you buried your muzzle between your paws. I knew you would be leaving soon." Airmead paused, then continued, "If it was not for the threat of this war, I might not have ever worked up the courage to go. A hundred times I promised that I would leave, but I was frightened to go alone. Don't worry. I was careful to cover my tracks and I left many false scents."

It hadn't even occurred to Katria to leave false scents; her head had been too filled with leaving. "I should have thought of that," Katria said. "I have been careful only to urinate in streams, though."

"That's good." Airmead paused. "I think we can make it, Katria. I think we have a chance. The chieftains and the lords are all caught up in this notion of capturing a grizzly cub, setting off a war between the wolves of the Watch and the bears." She sighed. "In my entire barren life as an Obea, I have never had to take a *malcadh* to a *tummfraw*. But I have to admit that the opposite thought did cross my mind." She stopped and cast her eyes down toward the ground. Snow had begun to fall, even though it was the first quarter of the Moon of the Flies.

"What's that?" Katria asked.

"I thought I might rescue that cub from Old Cags and perhaps stop a war."

"A single wolf is not going to stop a war," Katria said as she dug her claws deeper into the ground where the snow was beginning to stick. "Dunbar MacHeath will find another way. We must get to the MacNamaras and tell them what he's plotting. We don't have a lot of time. It is at least a four-day journey to MacNamara territory."

"Yes, but it will take Dunbar at least two days to get to where the cub dwells with his mother and then back to the Pit. And remember, the prevailing wind will be against them for part of the journey on their way to snatch the cub, and it will be with us for all of ours."

"True, but we have to move fast. Are you up to doing most of this journey at press-paw?"

"I'll try. I'm not an outflanker like you, Katria. I've never had to run a *byrrgis* and press in on the prey for leagues on end. And now this weather . . ." She hesitated. "If it snows again, it's going to be hard. But I'll try."

Airmead was right. It was going to be hard. Nearly impossible if there was another blizzard. Katria looked down. The snow was piled almost as high as the scar where her dewclaw had been. *Why are snowflakes dropping instead of flies during this moon?* Everything seemed turned around. Was there something worse than war coming?

CHAPTER FOURTEEN

THE SHE-WINDS

"PYGMY!" FAOLAN SHOUTED.

"Burrowing!" Edme said.

"Boreal!" they both blurted at once.

"Great Gray!" Faolan leaped a bit as the elderly *taiga* Malachy held up the jump bone with the incised profile of an owl's head.

"Long-eared!"

"No, Faolan," Malachy replied.

"Great Horned!" Edme said.

"Well, it had to be the other if not a Long-eared," Faolan said. "That was an easy guess."

"True." Edme nodded good-naturedly.

"It wasn't that easy," Malachy chided. "You forget Screech Owls have tufts as well. But now for the test," Malachy, a brindled wolf with crooked hips, said slyly.

"Edme, can you tell us the distinguishing characteristics between the so-called ears of the three species that sport them?"

"Uh . . . uh, I forget."

Faolan cocked his head. "I think," he began slowly, "that the Long-eared Owls' feather tufts stick up more and are closer together."

"Very good, Faolan. Yes, exactly, and the Great Horned Owls' tufts are wider apart and stick out at an angle. And the Screech's tufts are, well, somewhere in between." He paused and squinted at the two young wolves, a merry glint in his green eyes that reminded Faolan of the green sparkles on the river on a clear summer day. "Now, here's a tricky question for you."

"What's that?" said Edme, eagerly hoping to redeem herself with a truly challenging question.

"It has nothing to do with owls' heads."

"Uh-oh!" Edme and Faolan both said at once.

"Have a little faith in yourselves, young'uns. Which owl has featherless legs?"

"Featherless legs!" Edme said.

"Not a single feather!" Malachy snapped his jaws shut for emphasis. "Bare as a bear cub's butt."

Faolan and Edme inhaled sharply. "Uh," Edme

said, her voice taut. "Are you sure bear cubs' butts are bare?"

"Oh, yes, indeed. When they're first born. They hardly have a patch of fur on them. By the time they come out of the den, they're little fur balls. The cutest things you've ever seen. But never go near them; never touch them." Faolan and Edme grew very quiet, alarmingly quiet.

"Come on now, young'uns, the question isn't that hard. Which owl has no feathers on its legs?"

Faolan broke the silence. "Can you give us a hint?"

"Well, if you insist. I know you haven't seen that many owls because the volcanoes aren't very active yet, but which one did I tell you is the worst flyer?"

"The Burrowing Owl because . . . because . . ." Edme started to speak but was distracted by the thoughts of bear cubs. *Why did I play with that cub?*

"Because they're good at walking," Faolan said in a tentative voice.

"Exactly!" Malachy boomed. "Who needs feathers for walking or running?" He paused. "Anything wrong, young'uns?" He peered at them curiously. Their enthusiasm, their wonderful keenness, had suddenly vanished. Just then, a strange whining seeped into the den where

Malachy tutored new Watch wolves in the habits and customs of owls. He tipped his head. *Could it be?* It was strange it would come so early, but if that wasn't the peevish complaint of the She-Winds, well, he didn't have crooked hips.

"Hear that, young'uns?" he said softly but with great excitement.

At just that moment, a wolf came skidding down the chute into the den. "Hear that, Malachy?" It was Padraigh, wind scout for the Watch.

"Is it what I think it is?"

"It is, indeed. I've been as far south as the border of the Shadow Forest. It's the She-Winds. They're a-coming!"

"But it's not the season!" Malachy swayed a bit on his crooked hips, as if the very idea had unhinged him.

"She-Winds don't seem to mind none. They're back, and you know the owls can't be far behind them." He looked directly at Faolan and Edme. "Now your real larnin' begins, young'uns. No more jump bones. Real live owls on the wing!"

The She-Winds were unique to the Ring of Sacred Volcanoes. They seemed to arrive out of nowhere and go nowhere, but when they blew, they stirred the hot fluids in the deepest parts of the craters of all five volcanoes, and every Rogue smith and collier flocked to the Ring.

In the excitement of the moment, Faolan and Edme forgot their anxieties and followed Malachy and Padraigh out of the den. Twist and Winks came rushing up to them. "Your shifts are about to start. Get to your cairns."

The gusts were so strong that Faolan and Edme had trouble even standing straight at first. The ground beneath their paws shook as the first quaking belches of the volcanoes rumbled up from deep inside the earth. Faolan couldn't imagine how he was supposed to stay upright on his cairn, let alone perform the repertoire of scanning jumps they'd learned.

"Hang on to your fur, young'uns." Padraigh laughed raucously as he trotted away, angling himself to the winds that were lashing about them.

"Don't worry, we'll stay with you through your shifts," Twist said. "But regard Paddy — Padraigh — see how he is angling himself across the gusts." But Paddy always walked oddly. Of all the wolves of the Watch, his deformities were possibly the most curious. On one side, he was missing an ear, an eye, and a paw. It was as if he had been born lopsided, and yet despite his odd gait, he was effectively cutting through the maze of gusting winds that seemed to blow willy-nilly across the Ring, first from one direction and then another.

"The thing is, Faolan," Twist said as they reached the top of Stormfast's cairn, "I know these winds seem very confusing. But there's a peculiar order to them, which you'll see."

Faolan didn't see any order in the least. The air swirled not only with embers but with the grit scooped up from broken lava flows.

"Do you notice anything?" Twist asked eagerly.

"Yes, I notice that I'm having trouble standing upright."

"Tuck in your dewclaw and dig in with your others. Look. There are four nice femurs on the cairn, placed just so. Wrap your claws around them. We didn't place them that way just for the fun of it. Good gripping. Especially the bear femur."

"Bear?"

"Yes, there's a grizzly femur. Can't beat it for gripping."

Faolan's splayed paw was drawn to it by an invisible force. He knew that the bones in the cairns sometimes shifted, but why had he never seen this one before?

"Has this bone always been here?" Faolan cried out over the screech of the She-Winds.

"Oh, yes. It's what we call a keybone. It locks the whole cairn together. It never shifts."

"How come I never noticed it before?"

"Maybe you never really needed it before. But you'll see that it puts a spring in your leaps. Draw a bead on that bone. Fix it in your mind and it will keep you steady and your jumps true. Just feel it and picture it in your mind's eye."

And how he did feel that bone! It was as if he were experiencing a completely new way of seeing, as if his mind's eye were in his splayed paw. His first jump was not the best. He landed fine but didn't do the double inverted twist that would allow him to scan the entire rim of the crater and the sky above for graymalkins.

"I'm sorry," he said upon landing. "I didn't do that very well."

"It's challenging in these gusts. You see those owls flying in?"

"Yes, sir." Faolan had never seen so many owls before. They seemed to be pouring in from all directions.

"See how they are flying just off the wind? 'Crabbing,' they call it."

"Crabbing?"

"Yes, like a crab walking sideways, except they are flying. The wind is pushing them one way, away from their destination. So they angle their flight toward the direction of the wind. They are not really flying sideways, but instead of flying directly toward the slopes, they have slightly turned into the direction of the oncoming wind to compensate for the wind drift. The amount that the owls turn is called the wind correction angle. Now think about doing that when you jump."

"You mean I should jump into a gust."

"Yes, smack into it. And don't start your twists, flips, or pikes too soon or you'll miss the thermal drafts, and that's the great treat of leaping when the She-Winds blow." Twist looked up suddenly. "Look, Faolan! Look at that Masked Owl up there. By my marrow, I think it's your old friend Gwynneth — a lovely flyer if there ever was one."

"How does she do it?" Faolan was amazed. His dear friend appeared to be gliding effortlessly in the buffeting winds above, never even waggling a wing.

"She's riding the thermals, those billows of warm air. They lift the owls up high. A free ride, you might call it. And you can do it, too. We can't get as high as owls do, to 'owl point' as the term goes, but there's a place at the very top of a lifting draft that is known as the wolf's peak. Jump into a thermal and let it take you. It's the closest we wolves ever get to flying. Ready to try it?"

Faolan was so excited that his paws were almost dancing on the bones.

"All right. Now let's not rush this," Twist said. "When I say jump, you jump."

Faolan sensed the lead edge of a very hot gust.

"JUMP!" Twist shouted.

Suddenly, Faolan was rocketing into the air. It was so fast he barely had a chance to breathe. Embers whizzed by him like shooting stars. He had entered the sky, a peculiar firmament in which the constellations were composed of red swirling stars.

Faolan wasn't flying and yet he might have been. He had fur not feathers, legs not wings, and yet he felt a strangely familiar sensation — a stirring just where his shoulders joined his backbone. The billowing drafts of warm air caressed his underbelly and lifted him higher still. He wasn't as high as the owls, but he was in their world and it felt good. So good that he almost forgot to do any of the moves he had learned. So he drew up his hind legs for a backward walkover.

"Faolan! Welcome to the sky!"

"Gwynneth!"

She waggled her wings and flew off.

"Very nice, very nice indeed!" Twist said when Faolan landed back on the top of the cairn. "But you nearly forgot your scanning maneuvers."

"I know! I know!"

"Don't worry. It's a common thing for young Watch wolves when they first discover thermals. Look over there at Edme on Morgan. She's getting a lot of bounce out of them."

Yes, Faolan thought, *and she is managing several scanning moves — a double twist linked to a backflip.* Edme was not nearly as easily distracted as Faolan.

"What a jumper you are!" Gwynneth exclaimed as she alighted on the cairn. "A natural if I ever saw one." Faolan felt a surge of happiness stream through him.

"Well, I forgot to do any real scanning moves. It was just so . . . so . . . wonderful."

"You looked like you belonged up there with us."

"Really!" Faolan tipped his head to one side and looked deeply into Gwynneth's shiny dark eyes.

"Yes, really, Faolan. I never saw anything like it!"

After his shift was over, Faolan trotted happily back to the den. "Wasn't it fantastic, Edme?" he said, sliding down the slope into the den. "I mean, those drafts lift you right up. I felt it was as close as I'd ever come to flying like an owl —" He broke off mid-speech. "Edme?"

Edme was curled into a ball in a far corner with her muzzle buried between her paws. Absolute silence as loud as any noise engulfed the den.

"Edme, what is it?"

Without looking at him and with her muzzle still buried, Edme mumbled something in a muffled voice that Faolan had to strain to hear.

"You've been what?"

"Dalach'd," Edme said again.

"Dalach'd? No!"

"Yes. I can't jump for three nights."

"But why? What did you do?" Faolan asked.

"You know that arrangement of bones that they make so you can grip better?"

"Yes."

"I didn't show the proper reverence for the keybone."

"And so you got dalach'd? I mean, Twist never said anything about proper reverence. Did Winks tell you that?" Faolan asked, totally bewildered.

"It wasn't Winks. It was Banja. Winks wasn't feeling well."

"Banja — that old she-bag of a wolf!"

"She hates me, Faolan. I don't know why. I mean, she's missing one eye. If anything, she should understand me better, like Winks does. I'm not allowed on the cairn for the next three nights. How will I ever learn to navigate the She-Winds?"

"It's wrong. Completely wrong. Winks would never have done such a thing. I think we should protest," Faolan said staunchly.

"No, no. And it's my problem, not yours. I'm just going to try and forget about it." Edme circled her caribou pelt before she settled down again to try to sleep.

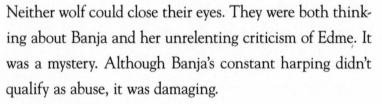

Neither wolf could close their eyes. They were both thinking about Banja and her unrelenting criticism of Edme. It was a mystery. Although Banja's constant harping didn't qualify as abuse, it was damaging.

"Faolan, you asleep yet?"

"No."

"Do you ever miss them?"

"Miss what?"

"The old days."

Faolan was on his feet in no time. "Edme, have you gone *cags*? Miss being a gnaw wolf? Miss the MacHeaths and the delightful time you had in that lovely clan!"

"No, not that. But you know, when we were all at the *gaddergnaw*. I think that was the best time of my life. Except for Heep, I really liked those other gnaw wolves — Creakle, Tearlach, the Whistler."

"I do miss the Whistler. He was —" Faolan paused. "He was something special, I think. I loved his voice. It was almost as if that hole in his throat . . . I don't know, drew in a special kind of air that made his howls so much more beautiful even though he kind of croaked when he talked."

Imagine, Faolan thought. *Banja has driven us to long for the awful old days when we were gnaw wolves.* And then he remembered two other wolves — Mhairie and her sister, Dearlea. By this time, Mhairie was probably a lead outflanker for the MacDuncans. Both of these sisters had come to his defense when he was wrongly accused of murdering a *malcadh* on the ridge, and then both of them cried with relief when he was exonerated of the crime and selected for the Watch. He was caught between the poles of two emotions — the sadness that comes when missing old friends, and anger at Banja that he was looking back with such wistfulness to a time marked by scorn and abuse.

"One last thing, Faolan," Edme said in a small voice.

"What?"

Edme hesitated. She had vowed that she wouldn't tell Faolan this, but it felt like a stone too heavy to carry alone.

"What?" Faolan asked again.

Edme sighed. "You know what she said when I didn't hit the keystone at the proper angle?"

"What?"

"She said, 'You and your friend Faolan are *moldwarpy* curs.'"

"What? She called us *moldwarps*?" *Moldwarp* was one of the most disparaging terms a wolf could use.

"Yes. I don't know what she has against you except that you're my friend."

"*Cag maglosc*," Faolan muttered, and then launched into what sounded to Edme like a string of Old Wolf curse words.

CHAPTER FIFTEEN

A TWINGE IN THE MARROW

TINY WHITE FLOWERS NO BIGGER than a pup's dewclaw bloomed out of the moss that clad the rocks of the Beyond. At night it seemed as if both the earth and the sky blossomed with stars. But the moss-flowers didn't last. The wind blew in an unseasonable snowstorm, which snuffed the flowers out.

At the Ring, there was incessant talk about the peculiar weather. The elders seemed worried, but Faolan was rather pleased, for the owls followed the She-Winds, and his learning took on a new dimension. He met owls, from Masked Owls to Great Grays, diving into the ember beds.

Although the weather was colder than usual for summer, Faolan rarely went to his and Edme's den when they were off duty. It was simply too interesting to hang about with the owls. Especially when a bird rarely seen in the Beyond arrived. She was a magpie who went by the name of Trader Luce and traveled with her assistant and a bundle of wares the likes of which neither Faolan nor Edme had ever seen.

"Where do they get all those . . . those . . ." Faolan grasped for a word to describe the strange objects. "Those things?" he finally blurted out.

"They belonged to the Others," Gwynneth replied. She noted the blank expression in the two wolves' eyes and sighed. "It's very hard to explain what the Others were."

"They *were*, not *are*?" Edme asked.

"Yes. They've been gone for thousands upon thousands of years."

"But what were they when they were?" Faolan asked.

"Well, to begin with, they didn't have wings," Gwynneth replied.

"Did they have legs?" Edme asked.

"Only two."

"What!" Edme and Faolan both shrieked.

"How could they get around on just two legs?" Faolan asked.

"Obviously not well if they've been gone for thousands of years," Edme replied.

"We only know about them because they left things behind." Gwynneth paused. "Let me take you down to meet Luce and you can see her 'merchandise,' as she calls it."

"Merchandise?" Faolan and Edme said.

Gwynneth shook her head wearily. "I think it's a term from the Others. Means 'stuff.' Come along, I'll introduce you. But for Glaux's sake, don't barter for anything. Luce would love to get her beak on some of your gnawed bones, I'm sure. You have to understand, for Luce, everything — and I mean *everything* — is merchandise." Faolan and Edme climbed down from the outcropping. Gwynneth was perched beside the magpie when they arrived.

"Luce, this is Faolan and Edme, new wolves of the Watch."

"Oh, my! So pleased to meet you, my dears. Can I interest you in anything?" She looked at them both and then focused on Edme's missing eye. "Mercy, I have just the thing for you! It's a false eye. Looks rather like a marble, doesn't it?"

Marbles, false eyes. Faolan's and Edme's heads were spinning.

Trader Luce held up a round white object with a bright blue center. "I only wish my dear granny had seen this. She was missing an eye like you, Edme. I'd give it to you for a gnawed bone. Not a femur or anything grand. A little tibia — a mouse's tibia would do."

"Stop it, Luce!" Gwynneth interrupted sharply. "You know it's forbidden for Watch wolves to trade bones. So get that idea out of your head right now."

"Sorry. I was just asking. Is that a new policy?"

"It's not a new policy. It's been around from time immemorial," Gwynneth snapped.

"Well, don't get all huffy about it." Luce turned away and squawked at her assistant, another magpie. "Dotty, bring those lace doilies over here on the double. Some gadfeathers might be flying in. They always go for that stuff."

Gadfeathers! Faolan had heard the word before, but now it stirred a little twinge in his marrow.

"Gadfeathers?" Edme asked. "What are gadfeathers, Gwynneth?"

"They sing!" Faolan said.

"Now, how ever did you know that, Faolan? I'm surprised."

Faolan looked startled.

"I think I heard one of the Watch wolves talking about it."

Gwynneth looked at him with curiosity, but continued, "They've become somewhat of a novelty. During ancient times in the northern kingdoms, there were countless gadfeathers. Recently, they've begun to come back. But very few have come into the Beyond, and that's why I was surprised when you said you'd heard of them."

Faolan said nothing. For the truth was that he was as puzzled as Gwynneth that he knew about gadfeathers and their singing.

Later, back on watch, Faolan stood atop Stormfast's cairn, peering into a sky draped with stars and the tracery of hot red embers. Would he know a gadfeather song if he heard one? But it was not only gadfeathers he wondered about. Some of his odd thoughts made him grip the keybone of the cairn more tightly than ever. He wanted to spring high into the night, catch the hottest of the drafts, and lift above the embers to the stars, as if they held the sources of the strange wisps of knowledge that came to him.

The night was torn with flames, and the red silhouettes of the volcanoes played across the barren landscape of the Ring. The shifting shadows of the night were like a scrim. On the other side, something was waiting for him, if he could only see it. A fate? A destiny only dimly perceived? Faolan sprang high, higher than he'd ever jumped before. The draft was hot, but he did not feel its heat. What he felt was cold, icy cold. *I am in a ring of fire, but I feel ice.*

PART THREE

THE CUB

CHAPTER SIXTEEN

OLD CAGS

TOBY HEARD THE LOUD SNORES
of his mother and the softer ones of his brother. It seemed
to the young cub that his mum and his brother, Burney,
spent all their time sleeping. Life was so boring. He wished
that nice wolf with one eye were here. But he hadn't seen
her since the day they'd played on the riverbank. She'd
taught him a game — hidey bone. He wanted to play it
again, but Burney never thought of interesting places to
hide the bone. And it was so exciting when the wolf ran
with it. She was so fast, but then could skid to a stop and
wheel about as quick as a wink. He decided to practice
now: At least that would be more fun than sleeping. So
he picked up a bone from a caribou his mum had taken
down earlier and began running with it.

Run, jump, quick turn, roll and up onto all fours, jump

again! Just as the little cub skidded to a stop, a gray she-wolf with black patches stepped out from behind a boulder.

"I can't believe it!" Toby cried with glee.

"Can't believe what, little one?"

"I was just hoping for a wolf to come play with me!"

"Well, how lucky we are, then." The she-wolf cocked her head to one side and regarded the cub. There was a hard glint in her eyes that stirred a pale shadow of unease in Toby, but he was so bored and eager to play.

"You like to play, don't you?" he asked.

"Oh, yes, most certainly," the wolf answered.

"Do you know the game hidey bone?"

"Why, yes. Now, where did a cub like you learn such a game?"

"From this wonderful wolf."

"Wonderful, she was? You don't say." The wolf grinned.

Toby was feeling a tad uncertain now. "Yes, wonderful. I just can't remember her name."

"What's your name?" the wolf asked.

"I . . . I . . ." *I shouldn't talk to strangers,* Toby thought as his mother's admonition came back to him. Fear and dread flooded through him. Every bristle of his fur prickled and stood up rigidly. Just then, four other wolves flashed out and surrounded him. Before Toby could even cry out, one of the wolves had clamped the cub's muzzle and lifted him off his feet.

"Think of this as a new game, dear." Fretta's voice threaded into Toby's ear. He could feel her warm, fetid breath on his face.

"My mum's going to be mad, reallllly really mad!" the little cub cried out when the wolves finally released the grip on his muzzle and he could scream. But it did him little good. He already knew that his mum and brother would never hear him. They were too far away by now, asleep on the riverbank. *Will they ever be sorry!* he thought.

At first there had been only one wolf. And she looked nice enough and Toby had remembered how he and his brother, Burney, had played with the one-eyed wolf earlier in the summer. That wolf was much younger and so much fun. This wolf was fun for about one second, and then three others had charged from behind a large boulder. Before he could even squeal, something had clamped down on his muzzle. He'd felt as if he were being lifted up, and the ground was just a blur rushing beneath him.

"All right, back off, Blyden," Fretta commanded. "You don't need to clamp his muzzle."

"She'll tear off your heads!" Toby shrieked. "That's easy for a grizzly. She'll rip out your heart and eat it! No, she'll just rip it out. She'd never eat such a foul heart."

Toby was a bright little cub and quite proud of his use of a fine word like "foul." He was scared, but he kept talking. Sometimes his mom said he talked too much. Burney was quiet, quiet and thoughtful. Toby was thoughtful but, well, noisy and thoughtful. "Would someone kindly answer me?" *Kindly?* he thought. What a poor choice of words with these thuggish wolves.

But at that moment, an owl swooped down with talons outstretched and started raking the wolves. Two of the wolves leaped up, taking swats at the owl, who quickly backed off. The wolves picked up Toby and streaked away.

They were transporting the cub by the scruff of his neck now. He hung down, his hind legs barely skimming the ground. He couldn't see the wolf carrying him, but four others ran alongside them. *I was just trying to have fun.* It was at that moment that he saw his own blood.

"Hey, I'm bleeding! You made me bleed."

"Shut him up! It was hard enough getting down here with the wind against us. I swear his yapping is slowing us down as much as the wind."

The she-wolf's jaws clamped down on Toby's muzzle. Everything within him turned dark with terror. He had to fight back somehow. They were bigger and stronger, but he had to do something even though he was scared. If he couldn't fight back with muscle, he would with words. He wriggled his muzzle free. "It's not just my mum who's going to get you. It's all the bears of the Beyond!"

"Precisely!" one wolf answered him.

Unbelievably, the wolves began to laugh.

Toby growled. "You think it's funny. It's not going to be funny, you poop balls!"

Toby was becoming more frightened by the minute. He had kept his eye on the sun as it sank toward the horizon and now his stomach clenched as they descended into a deep ravine that took a sudden plunge into a narrow pit. The wolf who had been carrying him dropped him in the middle of the pit and then scurried back to join the others, who stood on the embankment a fair distance off, watching with malicious anticipation. *What's going on here?* Toby thought, and then from a crack in the stone walls, a wolf staggered out. Frothy bubbles dribbled from his jaws.

Urskadamus! Toby thought. *A wolf with the foaming-mouth disease! They brought me to a wolf with the foaming-mouth disease!*

He knew there was no hope now. He would die a maddened cub in the most painful death imaginable. It would go on for days. His muscles would lock, his eyes would roll up in his head. His fur would get so hot, it would steam. He knew all about this disease. One of the first things grizzlies taught their cubs was never, ever, to go near a foaming-mouth animal — no matter what. Even if the sick animal were a grizzly, even if it were his own mother — she wouldn't recognize him and, in her madness, would only want to attack. What could he do? What could he do?

"Have a pleasant stay in the Pit," snarled one of his cubnappers.

"Shut your muzzle, Donaidh," snapped the largest of the wolves, who appeared to be their leader. He was a savage-looking creature with a horrible scar running down his face all the way to his neck. "I do the talking." The scarred wolf turned toward Toby and said in a dangerously soft voice, "What's your name, cubby?"

Cubby? The sound of the endearing word his mother often used when she nursed him made Toby want to puke. Toby remained silent. The scar-face wolf took a step toward him. "Your name?" His voice dropped and acquired an even more frightening edge.

"If he doesn't tell us his name, how will we —"

The scarred wolf wheeled around and bit the wolf Donaidh on his rump. "Shut up!"

But it was too late. Donaidh had given Toby an idea.

"Again and for the last time, what is your name?" the scarred wolf roared.

Toby replied in a quiet voice, "I don't have a name."

The she-wolf crept up to the scarred wolf. In a whisper, the she-wolf said, "I think we have to call him something. Old Cags can't keep much in his head, but you know how he is about names."

"We'll make up one. That should suffice," the gray wolf suggested.

"But he's a cub and not a pup. It could be confusing for Cags."

They actually bring pups to this pit! Toby thought. Who were these wolves? His mum had said that the wolves of the Ring were the best wolves of the Beyond, that forever and ever, they shared kills with bears, respected one another, and lived in peace. The wolves of the Ring were the wisest of all the wolves in the Beyond, and that is why his mum had decided to live near the Ring. But these were not good wolves!

Toby watched as the wolves conferred. They cast glances his way and then toward the foaming-mouth wolf. Toby had upset their plans by not giving them his name.

It seemed like a small thing. All he had done was refuse to speak. The talkative cub — indeed, his mother often scolded him for talking too much — had found richness in silence. The wind shifted and blew the words of the wolves closer, right into his ear. He tilted his head a bit more so he could hear better. Perhaps Great Ursus was looking out for him.

"But if we don't know his name, how do we let the news out that a cub has been stolen by the wolves of the Ring?" one wolf asked.

Stupid! Toby thought. Didn't they think his mum would miss him? Were these wolves so foul that they couldn't imagine how a mum would feel if her cub vanished?

"Let's make up a name — say Ian."

"Ian is a wolf name!" the scarred wolf snapped.

"Well, we don't know any bear names," the she-wolf said.

"Why don't you go ask him, Fretta. Just say, 'All right, could you give us another name to call you for now?'"

"I'll try."

Toby's mind raced as he saw the she-wolf Fretta trotting toward him. "Listen, you little —" She stopped herself. "I mean, listen, dearie." Never had a term of affection seemed more forced. "Cubby," she continued. The endearment dropped like sharp rocks from her mouth. "I suppose not telling your name is an old bear custom."

Brilliant! thought Toby. This idiot she-wolf had given him his best idea yet. He nodded.

"Can you tell me why?"

He tipped his head to one side thoughtfully, as if he were ruminating over a long, revered bear tradition.

Fretta looked at him inquisitively.

"It's unlucky."

"For you or me?" she asked.

Toby shrugged and gave an innocent *I don't know* look. *The joys of silence,* he thought.

"Well," Fretta continued, "we have to call you something. Could you help us out?"

He looked at her blankly.

"Give us a name, a sort of bearish name."

A bearish name! He thought a moment. He knew there was an opportunity here if he could just think of it. What if he didn't give a bearish name? What if he gave a very nonbearish name. Toby loved words, loved putting together odd-sounding parts of words. He and his brother, Burney, often made up nonsense just for fun. He was better at it than Burney. And how would these stupid wolves know what was bearish or not? *Ish . . . ish,* he thought. *Ish is funny-sounding.* It could be stuck on another odd sound. *Odd! I love that word!* he thought. *It's much better than weird or queer.*

"Listen," the scarred wolf said. "I don't want to waste any more time on this name thing. The trip already took half a day longer than we thought it would. The word will be out as soon as the mother starts yowling and thumping. We need time to prepare for —" But this time Toby cut Dunbar off.

"Call me Ishodd."

A sudden silence fell upon them. Dunbar snapped his jaws shut. The wolves seemed stunned.

What have I said? Toby wondered.

"Ishodd!" Fretta's green eyes nearly sprung from her head. "Why, that's a very . . . uh . . . wolfish-sounding — Old Wolf."

"Oh, really!" Toby opened his eyes wide. It was purely accidental, but he had to play along. He could tell that Fretta was greatly disturbed. "What does it mean in wolf?" he asked.

"I can't tell," she replied. Her legs were stiff and she'd shoved back in alarm. Fear seemed to radiate from her pelt.

"Unlucky, I guess," Toby replied quietly.

Fretta backed slowly away.

He watched her as she returned to the three other wolves. All their hackles had risen and their ears lay back flat against their heads. They turned to look at him, terror in their eyes. *What have I done?* Toby thought. *Can I get out of here? Will they let me go?*

In that same moment, it began to snow. The wolves looked up at the sky. "This is a bad business," said one wolf. "Remember what Edme said?"

"She's a fool," the leader growled.

Edme! That was the name of the wolf he had first played with. The one-eyed wolf had been so different from his attackers.

"But it is strange, my lord," Fretta said. "It snowed on Litha Eve and again now. Look, the sun is shining brightly and yet it snows." Her voice dropped. "The weather has gone *cag mag*, and the bear cub's name is Ishodd!" She stole a furtive glance at the foaming-mouth wolf weaving on his feet in the distance.

The scarred wolf looked up nervously at the sky.

Dunbar MacHeath came down from the safety of the embankment to grab Toby by the ear and drag him closer to the foaming-mouth wolf. When he released Toby, Dunbar streaked back up the embankment.

Toby immediately shut his eyes. The foaming-mouth wolf was the most frightening thing he had ever seen. His eyes were red, streaked with yellow. The gums of his diseased mouth were green, and Toby could smell the terrible stench of them.

"Old Cags, this is Macoon. Macoon, meet Old Cags! I'm sure you'll be friends. If you survive, Macoon."

"Macoon!" Toby's eyes flew open. "My name is not Macoon. It's Ishodd. Ish-odd!" He said it slowly, enjoying each syllable as all the wolves, including Old Cags, began to tremble.

Dunbar MacHeath let out a viscious snarl. "Say that again and I'll bite your ear off." But Toby didn't listen. He streaked across the pit and squashed himself into a crack in the rock walls.

Toby stayed inside this crack while the steep shadows of midday fell directly into the pit and then lengthened as the afternoon grew into night.

When the four wolves who had captured him left, Toby had heard them still muttering about his name. "Can you believe it? Ishodd. Of all the names!"

"What bad luck!"

"And now with this strange weather."

Why were they worried? His mum had told him that wolves were a very superstitious lot, not at all like bears. Had he stumbled across some sort of curse word or cursed name by accident? And why was it so important that the foaming-mouth wolf know his name?

Toby peered out from his hiding spot in the sheer rock wall. The old wolf was leaping about in the middle of the pit as if chasing his own tail. When he caught sight of Toby's muzzle, he bolted on a dead run toward the rock wall. *Surely it's not big enough for him to get in! Please, Ursus, take care of me. I don't want to die.*

There was a dull thud as the wolf slammed into the rock. He snarled, then began bellowing loudly. His language was garbled and there wasn't a word that Toby could understand. It was snarling gibberish. Again and again, the foaming-mouth wolf ran toward the crack. Then a sudden horrid odor suffused the air. Something slithered through the crack and into the narrow space, like a dark pink snake coated in yellow slime.

"Urskadamus!" Toby cried. It was Old Cag's long, fat tongue. The air reeked with disease. The tongue slithered toward Toby and he began to back away. He felt a sharp stone under his hind foot. Without even thinking, he grabbed it and slammed it down on the fetid slab of flesh.

There was a terrible yowl. Instantly, the tongue disappeared.

Toby's first sensation was not one of relief but fear. *That was stupid of me!* For he looked down and saw some dribbles of the deadly foam on the floor of the crack. He had gotten rid of Old Cags for now, but the sick wolf had left behind some of his disease. The glistening white bubbles seemed to wink at Toby in the dim light of the small space. He could catch the illness now and die, die without anyone ever knowing.

Shut up! he commanded himself. *Do something!* He dug his claws into the floor of his slot in the rock wall. The floor was not entirely rock. There was dirt, *earth!* The word blossomed in his mind like the most beautiful flower. Frantically, he began digging with his two front paws.

In no time, the deadly foam was buried under a pile of dirt. Toby looked around now for a rock. There was the stone he had slammed down on Old Cags, but he didn't want to touch that. Even though it had no foam on it, it was streaked with something that might have been blood. *I should bury it, too,* he thought. So he began digging again. After burying the foam and the rock, he peered into the back of the slot. Was there any chance, he wondered, that this crack went someplace? Could it be an escape tunnel? He felt along the walls and began to hope, for he had crawled quite a length, and the space had widened. But then his muzzle bumped up against a cold rock wall. A sickening feeling swam up in him. It was a dead end. There was no way out.

Outside he heard the wind blowing. It seemed to be growing colder. *Well*, he thought, *there is no sense staying in the back of this rock slot.* Old Cags must sleep sometime, and if Cags were sleeping, Toby could sneak out into the pit and see if he could find his way out. The pit was deep. He knew that. But the wolves had brought him down here by a path because wolves don't climb. *But bears do!* Toby thought. He and Burney climbed trees whenever they could find one. If he got a good look at the rock walls, maybe he could climb out of the pit.

Carefully, he approached the opening to the rock slot.

Another dead end! Old Cags certainly was sleeping — right by the opening. As soon as Toby peeked out, the wolf staggered to his feet, rushed toward the slot, and began snarling. Toby backed off. It was hopeless. And he could see that it was snowing much more heavily.

Toby shook his head as if trying to better compre-hend his dire situation. The snow sealed his fate, for if the snow moons had come early, the bears' cold sleep would soon begin. Toby's mum had told him and Burney about cold sleep. When the winter moons arrived, the bears would grow sleepier and sleepier, and their hunger would fade. The three of them would find a cozy winter den and all "lump up" together. He and Burney would nestle in their mum's thick fur and sleep until the very end of the last winter moon.

"But how can you not be hungry, Mum?" Toby had asked.

"You just aren't," she replied.

"But I always think about fish, the taste of salmon," Burney said.

"And I loved the moose liver we shared with the wolves," said Toby.

"And the spring onions," added Burney.

The two cubs had begun to name their favorite foods.

"You just forget," their mum replied. "You forget about food. You forget about everything, really."

Even me? Toby thought now. *Will they forget about me? Do they miss me? They must know now I'm gone, got lost or something. But if the cold comes, will they even forget about missing me?*

On the day Toby had been carried off, Burney had awakened from his nap. Before he even opened his eyes, he sensed that something was wrong. Very wrong!

"Mum, Mum. Wake up!"

"Burney, what are you doing waking me up so early from my nap? You and Toby go on and play. Let me get a bit more —"

"Mum, Toby's not here!"

"What?" Bronka's question came out more as a rumble than an actual word.

"He's gone, Mum. He always wakes up before me, but he's not here now!"

Bronka was up in a flash, galloping to the edge of the river and across the shallows to the bar. Toby couldn't have drowned. The water was too shallow and he knew how to swim. She clambered onto the bar and looked about. Then she saw the prints — wolf paw prints! She saw the scuffle marks and even some dark fur — her Toby's fur.

Burney stood in fear as he watched his mother's eyes

slide back in her head. There was a horrible renting bellow. She began the most awful roaring he had ever heard. Bronka heaved a huge boulder into the river and began pounding her feet and paws.

"My child, my cub, my cub! The wolves stole my cub! I'll tear their heads off! I'll tear off their legs and gouge out their eyes!"

"Mum! Mum!" Burney cried out. He was so scared, but she could not hear him through the roaring din and the thunderous pounding of her massive feet. .

A league or more down the river, another grizzly mother heard the rage of a mother whose cub had been taken, wounded, or killed. Instinctively, she reached for her tiny cub and pressed him close to her chest.

"Mum! Mum you're squeezing me too hard!"

She licked his muzzle with her warm tongue. "Hush! Hush, little cub."

CHAPTER SEVENTEEN

SHADOWS OF WAR

KATRIA AND AIRMEAD HAD BEEN traveling at press-paw speed. They now were standing on the edge of the shore of the Sea of Hoolemere. The fog rolled in from the southeast across the inlet, known as the bight, where a narrow strip of land hooked out and into the choppy water.

"Broken Talon Point," Katria said. "We could save half a day at least if we swam this inlet. And the current would be with us, along with the wind." She turned her head slowly toward Airmead. "Do you swim?"

"What wolf doesn't?" She chuckled.

"It'll be cold."

"We have fur."

"Our fur might freeze when we get out and the wind hits us. Ice will add weight."

"We'll shake the water off," Airmead said. She was already striding into the water.

"It won't be easy. I just want to warn you," Katria called after her.

"Living with the MacHeaths isn't easy either. I'd rather die at the bottom of the Sea of Hoolemere than in the clan of the MacHeaths."

That did it — Katria leaped into the churning waters of the inlet. The current was with them and it was strong. It almost seemed as if they couldn't paddle their legs fast enough to keep up with it. The hardest part was holding their heads above the slapping waves. The fur on their face was soon rimed with salt. When they were about two-thirds of the way across, they began to feel themselves being pulled south.

"What's happening?" Katria said.

"There must be an eddy swirling out from the shore."

The eddy was dragging them fast now. They were swimming as hard as they could, for they were in real danger of being swept past the point and straight out to sea.

"Swim! Swim!" Katria yelled. She was younger and much stronger than Airmead. She could see Airmead's head drooping and the water dashing in her face.

Katria, too, was having to fight hard. She did not have breath to spare, but she shouted out, "Airmead! Think of the MacHeaths and then think of life. Life, Airmead!" The words of the *banuil caints* flowed through her mind, words from bones that she had long forgotten but now seemed inscribed in her marrow. *You are good. You are wise. You have strengths you have never known.* And she shouted out all of the words she had found on those buried bones, until the salt air seemed to sing with them. She felt a surge within herself and she saw that Airmead was lifting her head higher. It was as if there were three powers propelling them toward the shore of Broken Talon Point — the wind, the current, and the secret language of Hordweard.

When Katria and Airmead staggered out of the water, they knew they had only a short distance to travel, another day at the most. They had cut a four-day journey into one that would barely take them three. Although they should have been exhausted, they found themselves oddly invigorated, and pressed on at almost attack speed. Their stops for rest were brief. Their food was restricted to prey nearby, small creatures that barely satisfied their hunger but were easy to catch. They had set out from the MacHeaths with a surge of energy that came with their sense of release, of deliverance from constant fear and savagery. But like the stench from a foul place, the brutality of the MacHeath plan to snatch a cub and take him to the Pit clung to them every step they took. Could they get to the MacNamaras in time? Could a cub be saved and a war averted? These questions drove them to a relentless pace.

When they finally slowed, Airmead noticed something. "What a strange track," she said, looking up at Katria.

"How so?" Katria came over to where Airmead was standing. Katria lowered her muzzle to the prints that were blurred in the mud. The snow had ceased, the sun had come out and melted any remains of it, but the air was colder. That made sense, for they were far north, as far to the northeast as they had ever been. The previous day, they'd crossed the Broken Talon Peninsula, and by nightfall at the latest they would be with the MacNamara pack. By now, they were at least a hundred leagues from MacHeath territory. With each league, they had felt freer and a bit safer, for twice it had snowed and covered their tracks. They were both thankful for this strange weather, so peculiar to the summer moons. But then ahead of them, they had caught sight of paw prints.

"It's an outflanker's print!" Katria said.

"An outflanker's!"

"Absolutely."

Airmead would not question her word because Katria herself had long served as an outflanker for the MacHeaths, first in her natal pack and then in the pack of the chieftain when she had joined with Donaidh.

"But she . . ." Katria stopped.

"What? She what?"

"Something is wrong with her."

"Not the foaming-mouth disease. Her paw mark is straight," Airmead said quickly. A splayed paw print was the sign of the disease.

"No, no, it's not splayed at all. And the scent is not MacHeath. I want to backtrack a bit and look at the prints more closely. You can wait here. I'm not going far," Katria said.

Airmead settled down on a soft clump of rabbit-ear moss. She knew that the owls sometimes used this moss to line their nests. She looked at Katria as she quickly loped down the trail, her gait easy and efficient. The MacHeaths would miss her as an outflanker. Katria was not given to much talk, but she was obviously still grieving for her daughter, Kyran. That would pass. Perhaps she would find a new mate in the MacNamara clan and have a new litter. How lovely to raise pups free from the brutality and terror of the MacHeaths. She herself could have no such dreams, of course, for she was barren.

It wasn't long before Katria returned. "I think she's blind."

"Who's blind?"

"The outflanker. She's being led."

"I can understand how you can tell that she is being led. I mean, there are other wolf's prints up ahead. But how can you tell she's blind?"

"It's hard to explain. There's a certain hesitation before she puts down her lead paw, and she plants it too hard. As if . . . as if . . . she thinks the earth might slip out from under her."

Airmead nodded. "Let's get on our way."

"Yes, we might catch up with them."

It was nearing noon when they spotted the two wolves. As they rounded a bend, a wolf with a pelt the color of cooling flames stepped out from a thin stand of trees.

Airmead and Katria immediately began the submission postures.

The red wolf blinked. *MacHeath she-wolves,* he thought. No other wolves would begin submission postures so far in advance. They were now crawling on their bellies toward him. One of them had powerful shoulders, and he could tell she had been an outflanker. He trotted up to greet them.

"Please, please, rise up. No need for such observances here." He spoke in a kind, respectful voice.

Airmead and Katria stole glances at each other. They were not used to such greetings. Slowly they rose to their knees but kept their tails low and their ears pressed back demurely.

"I am Brangwen, out of·the MacDonegal clan."

"Oh, my," Katria said. "You have come a long way."

"Yes. My mate . . ." He tossed his head in the direction of the stand of trees. "You see she is not well." He hesitated, then said in a trembling voice that nearly broke Airmead's and Katria's hearts, "She . . . she's blind."

"And she was an outflanker," Katria said softly.

"Yes." Brangwen nodded, lifting his eyes to Katria. "You could tell, couldn't you? Because you're one as well."

"Yes."

"I thought so. Your shoulders." Katria said nothing. "My wife, Morag, had a lot of good years left in her until the blindness came to her. We had to leave. There's no place for an outflanker who can't . . . can't . . ."

"I understand," Katria said. "You seek the Mac-Namaras. They make room for such females."

"Yes, and you two seek the MacNamaras and don't need to explain why, either." He paused, then said in a more buoyant voice, "Come, let me introduce you to Morag. She'll enjoy meeting a fellow outflanker and her friend." He nodded at Airmead.

Airmead was struck by this wolf's gentle manners. How kind of him to include her — she who was no use at all to anyone. She was an Obea, and most wolves, MacHeaths or otherwise, looked skittishly at barren females. Especially other she-wolves. She was thankful that Brangwen's mate, Morag, was blind and might not sense her barren state. But then again, it was said that blind animals' awareness of smell was sharper than creatures who could see.

Airmead didn't need to worry. Morag seemed only happy to meet the two MacHeath she-wolves. She betrayed no sign of sensing that Airmead had been an Obea. There was not the slightest twitch of her nostrils to indicate that she'd picked up a whiff of Airmead's sterility.

"Well," Morag said. "A clan can always use another

outflanker. I'm not sure what they'll do with me." She spoke in an almost cheerful manner.

"Now, my dear, you can't see," Brangwen offered, "but you'll be a good auntie." Aunting behavior was common among wolves. If a she-wolf was too busy to mind her pups, another she-wolf often stepped in.

"I'm a good auntie because as an outflanker I had to depend on other good aunts when I was out on *byrrgis*. I appreciate what they did for my pups." A shadow passed through Morag's eyes and there was the dimmest pulse of green behind the milky film that covered them.

"No one can tell stories to pups like Morag," Brangwen continued. "She has a true gift for the old ones, the stories of the Long Ago."

Both Katria's and Airmead's tails drooped. There was rarely any storytelling among the MacHeaths. They did not value the tales of the Long Ago, when the wolves had first arrived after the Ice March. They lived only in the strife-torn depravity of their own here and now, smug in their ignorance of the past and the rich lore of the wolves of the Beyond. The MacHeaths didn't even have a proper *skreeleen*. One of the tasks of a *skreeleen* was to read the sky fire to tell stories. The MacHeaths only had one ancient, nasty female whose sole tasks were to croak out territorial boundaries and announce what prey was in the region.

The four wolves returned to the trail. Morag seemed to gain confidence in the company of strong she-wolves, and Brangwen noticed that her pace had picked up. Airmead trotted behind Morag, and Katria was right at her shoulder, gently guiding her just as she might have initiated a flanking action to bend a *byrrgis* on the hunt.

"We must be nearing the camp," Brangwen called out. "Look at this fog rolling in. We're close to the northern sea. The Bittersea, I believe they call it."

Mist began threading the air and quickly they were enveloped in an immense cloud that seemed to have settled across the land. The tips of their guard hairs were soon bristling with drops of vapor, and their pace slowed.

"How come we're going slower?" Morag asked.

"The fog. We can't see much."

"Maybe I should lead." Morag chuckled good-naturedly. Katria and Airmead gasped.

"What are you gasping about?" Morag asked.

"You made a . . . a . . ."

"A joke?" Morag asked.

"Yes. Is that what you call it? A joke?"

"Yes. Great Lupus, haven't you ever heard anyone make a joke before?"

"No," Katria and Airmead answered at once.

"Not in the MacHeath clan," Airmead clarified.

"And certainly not about one's self," Katria added.

"Well, that's . . . that's too bad," Morag replied. She could think of nothing else to say.

A short time later, the fog rolled out again and they caught sight of two wolves coming toward them. "Scouts!" Brangwen exclaimed. "They must be scouts from the MacNamara clan."

"You mean we've arrived?" Morag said.

Brangwen began to howl a greeting and when the scouts drew close, the four traveling companions fell to their knees and began the submission postures.

They were cut short as Brangwen had cut short Katria and Airmead. A large she-wolf with a creamy gray pelt that looked almost like her own private fog stepped forward.

"Welcome. You are welcome. We have seen you coming since dawn. I must apologize for the Namara. She regretted that she was unable to greet you personally.

She usually does, but I am afraid you have arrived on the eve of what might be a catastrophe."

"A catastrophe?" Brangwen asked.

"Oh, dear," whispered Morag.

"What is the trouble?" Katria asked.

"The bears — the bears near the Ring are rising up against the wolves."

"But we've always lived in peace with the bears, especially in the territory of the Ring. This is impossible!" Brangwen said.

"Let's hope," said the other scout, a dark gray male. "Let's hope," he repeated.

Katria and Airmead exchanged glances, and Katria began to speak. "We know something of this. I'm ashamed to say that we did little to stop it. It's the MacHeaths' doing, and it's why we finally gained the courage to leave." Katria paused.

The scout shoved her ears forward. "You must come with me directly and tell what you know to the Namara. Perhaps you can help us avoid . . . this . . . this . . ." She was hesitant to say the word that hung unspoken in the air. "Please just follow me."

Morag in her blindness sensed a deeper darkness — the shadow of war.

CHAPTER EIGHTEEN

GRAYMALKIN

IT WAS FAOLAN'S SECOND DOU-
ble shift, and then he had been promised two nights off
entirely. Something was going on at the Ring, but neither
he nor Edme was sure quite what it was. As new members
of the Watch, they were not included in the *gaddergovern*, the meetings in which business matters of the Watch
were discussed. But tempers were short, and even the ever-
patient Twistling was snappish with Faolan.

The She-Winds had abated and fewer owls were
streaming in. It was mostly Rogue smiths who had stayed
to tend the temporary forges they had set up.

Gwynneth had stayed, and for this Faolan was deeply
grateful. He and Edme had learned almost as much from
Gwynneth as they had from Malachy, the *taiga* who spe-
cialized in owl studies. It was Gwynneth who really made

them feel what it was like to live an owl's life, even though she was a hermit and lived mostly in the Beyond.

But Gwynneth seemed to know less about what was going on at the Ring than they did.

"Double shifts?" she had asked with mild surprise. "Now that the She-Winds are lessening, I can't figure out why that would be necessary."

"Yes. See, there's Edme. She's just leaving her cairn by Morgan — and late at that. Her replacement must have been delayed. It seems like the *taigas* are always in a *gaddergovern* with the Fengo or some other high-ranking Watch lords." Faolan paused. "Could you find out anything, maybe?" Faolan asked in a beseeching tone that Gwynneth had never heard him use.

"Absolutely not! You're asking me to gizzle!"

"Gizzle? What's that?"

"To sneak in and hear something. Thus the name slipgizzle. In short, spy!" Gwynneth spat out the word. "Their stock-in-trade is information. I have no time or trust for such owls. I am no slipgizzle!"

"I didn't say you were," he replied. "I have to get back to my jumps."

"Don't be angry," Gwynneth said, suddenly contrite. "I tend to go off a bit about slipgizzles. They have their place in owl society. And they've done a lot of good. The Great Tree is very dependent on them."

"All right. I'm sorry I asked you."

"Don't worry," Gwynneth said as she began to spread her wings. Effortlessly, she lifted into flight.

As so often happened when Faolan stood close to owls or watched them take off into the sky, he seemed to feel stirrings deep within him, whispers from another time or another world. But it wasn't just when he watched owls. These whispers had started coming to him during his *Slaan Leat*, his journey toward truth. There was a truth out there still waiting for him, and every once in a while, he caught a glimpse of it. Sometimes when he did his leaps, especially the high ones where he rode the warm drifts to wolf's peak, he felt as though he was coming close to catching mists or wraiths from the past.

Owls called them scrooms, wolves mist or *lochin*. These mists from an unreachable past seemed to seep through his mind. He felt sometimes as if he were trespassing on someone else's memories or dreams. But it was not his fault. He could never quite figure out what prompted these moments. And when they occurred, he felt as if he were a wolf out of time.

When he had completed his scanning jump and

landed back on the cairn, he looked down and spotted Edme.

"Going off duty?" he asked. Edme looked up at him.

"Yes, finally!"

"I'm on until dawn. Why aren't you back in the den already asleep?"

"I don't know. I find it hard to sleep. It seems like the whole Ring is holding its breath and nobody is telling us anything."

"It's not just us. Gwynneth came by and she doesn't know any more than we do." Faolan tipped his head skyward, scanning for graymalkins. From the corner of one eye, he caught sight of a Spotted Owl lingering low in the sky on the southeastern edge of the crater. He felt a funny twitch in his marrow. Was this owl cratering? Should he howl the graymalkin alarm? He listened for the brittle crunching that was said sometimes to emanate from the crater when a graymalkin approached, but he heard nothing. False alarms were not looked upon kindly. Besides, it was not really the season for graymalkins. They usually came with the She-Winds, flying under the camouflage of the throngs of colliers and Rogue smiths streaming in. Still he was nervous.

"I'm going up!" he said to Edme. "Wait here."

Edme was so tired by this point that she could not have managed a hop. So she settled herself on the cairn's platform and tipped her head to follow Faolan's jump.

He was a magnificent jumper, no doubt about it. The tales of when he leaped over a wall of fire had swept across the Beyond. She had not witnessed it, but those who did had said they'd never seen anything like it. That alone should have qualified him for the Ring.

"What in the name of Glaux!" Edme muttered as she looked up. She had begun to take up many of the owl expressions and milder swear words. She watched Faolan reach out and grab what looked like an ordinary Spotted Owl. Before she could wonder, Faolan was back on top of the cairn.

He dropped the owl and quickly pinned it down with his starboard forepaw.

"I didn't mean to! Honest, I didn't mean it!" The owl was hysterical.

"Faolan, a graymalkin!"

"I think so."

"Well, why didn't you howl the alarm?"

Faolan looked at her blankly. "I'm not really sure."

"That's unconscionable! You could get into a lot of trouble."

"I didn't want to send a false alarm. I just thought there was something —"

"Don't, don't, don't! Please don't sound any alarm," the owl pleaded.

"Why were you hanging around over the crater? There weren't any coals shooting out. The She-Winds are gone. What's your excuse?" Faolan's voice was rising.

"All right, all right. I just . . . I just . . ." the owl sputtered.

"You just what?" Edme stomped down on his other wing.

"I did it on a dare," the Spotted Owl blurted out.

"A dare!" Faolan said. "Are you *yoicks*?"

"Yes, definitely. I am completely, totally, eternally *yoicks*."

"But why?" Edme asked.

"I was sick of them making fun of me. I wasn't really going to take the ember if I saw it. But Skylar said that sometimes after the She-Winds blow out, you can see the ember float to the top."

"Skylar is full of wet poop!" Faolan said. This was one of the nastier owl curses because owls prided themselves on their discreet and noble digestive systems, which allowed them to produce neatly packaged pellets, unlike other birds who excreted white splats.

"Probably, but I just wanted . . . well, you know, for them . . . to like me. I fly funny. You saw it. That's why you caught me so easily. My port wing tip is turned funny."

"That is no excuse! Look at Edme. She has one eye. Look at me." Faolan shifted his weight so he could hold down the Spotted Owl's wing and lift up his splayed paw. "Have a look, idiot!"

"That's, uh, some paw!"

"It certainly is. And I've learned to live with it — very well, I might add — as Edme has learned to live with one eye. And guess what else?"

"What?" the owl asked in a trembling voice.

"We were never accepted until we came here. We were gnaw wolves, bitten and beaten up, the last ones at the kill allowed to eat."

"I'm really sorry."

"Sorry!" Edme exclaimed with contempt.

"Are you going to howl the alarm?"

"We should," Faolan replied.

"No, you shouldn't," the owl said quickly.

"Why not?" Faolan asked.

"Because I know something . . . something important." His yellow eyes had a sudden crafty shimmer. "I know about a cubnapping!"

As the moon moved across the night and began its slide down the western sky, the owl, whose name was Arthur, told the story of what he had seen.

"I was just minding my own business, flying with a Fish Owl over the river, looking for trout. And I saw this little cub — a cute little fellow." Edme felt her legs begin to wobble, as if her bones had sprung a leak and her marrow were dribbling away. Faolan, too, felt a darkness run through him.

"Go on," Faolan said. "You saw a cub."

"Well, yes, and a wolf stepped out from behind a rock, and the little cub trotted right up to the wolf and wanted to play! Play, I tell you! A baby cub and a wolf."

"The wolf — what did he look like?" Edme asked weakly.

"It wasn't a he. It was a she. She was gray with some patches of black."

"Did she have a white-tipped tail?"

"Yes! Yes, as a matter of fact!"

"Fretta." Edme whispered the name. "She's a scout for the MacHeaths."

Arthur squirmed a bit. "Hey, how about letting up a

little with that foot of yours? You're squashing my plum-mels to bits!"

"Go on!" Edme said impatiently.

"So this she-wolf steps out, and at first she seems really nice, but suddenly three more wolves step out from behind the rock. One was pretty ugly. Uglier than you," he said, glancing toward Edme. "Ouch!" Faolan had pressed down sharply on the wing. "You want to break my wing or what?"

"Don't call her ugly! You're the ugly one, to take a dare! Great Glaux!"

"Oh, be quiet, Faolan!" Edme snapped. "I don't give a white splat of seagull poop what this creature calls me. Go on with your story."

"Sorry," Arthur said. "Anyhow, it all happened so fast. Two of the wolves pounced on the cub, the other two rushed in, and before you knew it, the cub was being car-ried away. And . . . and . . ."

"And what?" Edme asked.

"Well," Arthur said hesitantly, then just blurted it out. "The Fish Owl, Skylar, he was really courageous and he started to dive-bomb them. But I was scared. I was a coward." It all became very clear now to both Faolan and Edme.

"Because you were a coward and didn't attack as your friend Skylar did, you felt you had to prove yourself. And so you took the dare to find the Ember of Hoole," Edme said.

The Spotted Owl remained silent.

"That about sums it up, Edme," Faolan replied with contempt.

"No, not exactly," Arthur said in a small voice.

"What do you mean 'not exactly'?" Edme asked.

"The bears know about it now. There's talk of a war between the wolves of the Beyond and the bears."

"No!" Faolan gasped. "It can't be."

"I think he's right, Faolan. That's the answer to the double shifts and all the meetings in the *gaddergovern*. Arthur, when did you see the cubnapping?"

"Two days ago. The wolves here probably just found out yesterday."

"It doesn't matter — yesterday, today, there can't be war. There just can't be," Faolan whispered hoarsely.

"Why wouldn't the *taigas* tell us?" Edme wondered aloud. Then it dawned on her. She looked at Faolan. "It's you, Faolan."

"Of course it's me," he replied in a low voice. His eyes filled with tears. "They were trying to protect me."

"Why?" Arthur asked.

"My second Milk Giver was a grizzly. Her name was Thunderheart."

"What?" The Spotted Owl could barely get his beak around the word.

"Yes. She saved my life. A grizzly bear saved my life."

Arthur was silent for several seconds as he attempted to digest this extraordinary information. Then pulling himself up a little taller and squaring his shoulder feathers, he spoke: "I might be able to help you — just a bit."

"You? How? You're a coward, remember?" Faolan snapped. Edme nosed him in his flank.

"Be quiet, Faolan. Let him speak. How can you help us, Arthur?"

"I know where they took the cub. Skylar and I followed them."

"So where did they take him?" Edme asked.

"A box canyon with steep walls on all its sides. There's a hidden trail through the brush down into it and . . ." His voice dwindled away.

Edme lifted her single eye to Faolan and spoke. "And there's a crazy old wolf living down there with the foaming-mouth disease. The Pit. That's where they took the cub."

"Do I get to go, now that I've told you everything?" Arthur asked.

Edme stepped up to the owl and met his gaze directly. "Not quite yet, Arthur. This is your chance to redeem yourself and prove your courage. This is not a dare, this is an order. Think of yourself as a soldier in the first skirmish of the war between the bears and the wolves."

"But I'm not a wolf," he replied in a whiny voice.

Edme gave a resounding swat to the owl's face, smacking off a few feathers, which drifted up and then settled on the cairn. Faolan had never seen Edme display such temper. "Let me knock some sense into you, dear," Edme said. "The owls are going to be dragged into this war. So it doesn't matter if you're not a bear or a wolf or an owl. The important thing is not to be an ass. You're going to fly cover for us. Got it?"

But first, Faolan and Edme knew they must go to the Fengo.

CHAPTER NINETEEN

KILLING FEAR

THE PROBLEM IS THE NAME, CAGS thought in his feverish and disorderly mind. *Yes, that's the problem.* There were two names the wolves had called this pup who did not look like a pup. Was he really a pup? Cags needed a name. He liked to call out the pup's name, hear it bounce off the walls. It was as if the name crawled around inside the pup's head, and the pup's brain got all twisted up, like Cags's. It got foamy.

But if Old Cags didn't have a name, he couldn't focus. And if he couldn't focus, his terror shrank to the size of a dried-up peaberry in the hunger moons. Old Cags fed on terror — the terror that he could create. But he didn't know what to do without a true name. So he walked back and forth in front of the rock wall where the pup who was not a pup had hidden himself in a crack.

Old Cags's job was either to scare a pup to death or into a kind of mute insanity. Sometimes the pups who came to him died of hunger if they couldn't find the mice and rats that lived in the Pit, and sometimes they just plain gave up and ran directly at him. Then he would bite at them with his back teeth, which was actually hard for him to do since he had no fangs left, and the pup would die foaming. Cags had not died for some strange reason, and that made him special. The chieftain told him so. He was almost like a god in the eyes of the MacHeaths, a god who must live separately in his stone heaven.

It was no fun for Cags when a pup charged him and he bit it. It was all over too quickly. Even their dying became boring if it lasted too long. Sometimes Cags envied their death throes — their lives had ended, their fear was finished, and their loneliness was over. They could begin to climb the star ladder, which he seemed never to reach in his living death.

The best was when a pup became what Old Cags called stony-eyed and he could make it do his bidding. The pup could chase red squirrels and kill them so Old Cags could eat. He much preferred the taste of red squirrels to rats. And then when the chieftain came, he would praise Old Cags. "You always turn out an obedient pup, dear Cags," he would say. "No more trouble from this one." The pup would leave, his eyes as smooth and lifeless as river pebbles.

Toby peered out from the crack he was squashed into. If he retreated to the rear of the slot, there was more room and he could be more comfortable. But he had to keep a watch on the foaming-mouth wolf. He had found a few mice to eat, but he was too frightened to be hungry. He shook so hard with fear as he watched Old Cags coming closer to the rock wall that he thought his fur might fall off. In fact, his pelt had begun to shed and he simply hadn't noticed it, until a breeze blew into the cave and he saw filaments of his own dark brown fur swirl up into the dim light. He looked around and inhaled sharply. The small stump of his tail was bare, with pink skin showing through. First he was shocked by the stupid pink stub that looked as if it had been tacked to his butt with sticky gum from a pine tree, and then he got mad. And when he got mad, it was as if something inside him broke in two. Part of him was still a baby seeking his mother's comfort, and the other part was not a cub any longer. *You have to grow up! Grow up! Don't cry. Think!* In his mind's eye, a picture formed of his baby self saying good-bye to the cub he was becoming.

Toby pressed his face against the crack and looked out at Old Cags, who was staggering about, muttering something. *It's just me and Old Cags,* Toby thought to himself. *No,* he corrected with a sudden burst of inspiration. *It's not just me and Old Cags. It's me, Old Cags, and fear.* Fear was as much a part of their small company as anything. Fear was alive, with a heartbeat of its own. There were three living things brought together in this stone prison, and one of them had to die. Toby decided to kill fear.

His first task was to listen carefully to try to understand what Old Cags was muttering about. He tried as best he could, but all he could decipher was something about names. Dare he step outside just a bit?

He inched out from the crack for the first time since he had found it. A blade of moonlight sliced across the ground, and he felt the cold, harsh wind on his ridiculous pink stub. Just thinking of his tail made him mad.

Old Cags regarded him with a dazed look. Toby held his breath, but Cags did not charge.

"Whazz name?" The words slurred.

"I told you already."

"They said two names." He swung his head back and forth, his eyes spinning and a small cataract of foam spilling onto the ground. "Need name."

If he needs it, I'm not giving it to him, Toby thought. That would be his first move. So he said simply, "I have no name."

Confusion swam in the sick wolf's eyes. He lay down and buried his muzzle in his paws.

Toby had just put the first nick in the pelt of fear.

CHAPTER TWENTY

BREAKING RULES

"HOW DID YOU FIND THIS OUT? Who told you about the impending war and the cubnapping?" Finbar was fuming, but Faolan could tell that the cubnapping was not news to him.

"It's out there. Gossip. I heard the owls talking about it."

"The owls don't know a thing."

This was true, but Faolan could hardly say it was a graymalkin who was the source of his information, because he would be in trouble for not sounding the alarm. And in truth, he hardly thought of Arthur as a real graymalkin. He seemed more like a confused youngster than anything else. But Faolan could be dismissed from the Ring if they discovered he had spoken to a graymalkin and had not sounded the howl alarm.

Faolan had also not yet mentioned that he knew where the bear cub was being kept. If the foaming-mouth wolf bit anyone from the Watch, the disease would spread like wildfire. The fewer who went to the Pit, the better. Faolan's intention had been to say that he would like to go talk to the bears, and not mention his and Edme's plan to rescue the cub. But he wasn't sure how to introduce the notion of a parley with the bears.

Faolan would do anything to stop the war. He couldn't tolerate the idea of going against the bears, his second Milk Giver's species. It was like making war on himself. *I will die before one drop of grizzly blood is shed.*

Jasper, a dark brown wolf who was the highest-ranking wolf of the Watch after Fengo, now stepped forward. One of his hind legs was half the length of the others and ended not in a paw but in a knob with claws sticking out of it every which way.

Jasper always spoke slowly as if he were turning over each word before uttering it. "Now . . . young'un . . . this is a council of war. Whatever makes you think that you belong in this cave? You've been here, what" — he looked around with a musing air — "one moon, certainly less than two, and you feel that you have the right to interrupt this meeting. What could you possibly contribute in this situation?"

Faolan was growing desperate. He would have to tell them he knew where the cub was being held. But it was Edme who stepped forward. She looked up with her single eye into Jasper's large and handsome face.

"Sir, I was a MacHeath. I know where they took this poor cub." The cave grew still. "They took him to the Pit."

"The Pit? You mean it really exists?"

"Yes. It does. It's a terrible place. Let Faolan and me go after the cub." She was careful not to mention Arthur.

Thank Lupus, Faolan thought.

"I know the ways of the MacHeaths, and Faolan knows the ways of bears," Edme continued.

"But it will be dangerous for the two of you," the Fengo said. "Is there truly a foaming-mouth wolf in the Pit?"

"Yes. But the danger of the Pit is nothing compared to the danger of a war between the bears and the wolves. If we can save that cub . . ."

"I see what you are saying." Finbar paused and thought for several seconds before speaking again. "I have been informed," he said, "that the cub snatched was not any mere cub but the great-grandson of none other than Grizz, the Bear of Bears." There were gasps as the wolves absorbed this latest information. "Yes, so you can understand how truly dire this situation is. Scouts have already brought in reports of the bears massing. If they attack, we shall have no choice but to defend ourselves. Therefore, I think it is wise that Edme and Faolan go to the Pit immediately and try to rescue the cub. But, by Lupus, be careful! If one of you is bitten, the other must leave you to die alone. The disease must not be spread. In the meantime, our *raghnaid* will go and seek to parley with the bears. If you can bring the poor cub back in time, we might be able to avoid war."

Banja now stepped forward. "I do not think it is at all advisable that we permit Edme to go on this mission. She is, after all, a MacHeath. Suppose she decides to join them."

"What!!" Edme and Faolan both barked in astonishment. The Fengo himself seemed to stagger upon hearing Banja's words.

Every hair on Edme's pelt stood up and she suddenly seemed twice her size. "Are you accusing me of being a turnpelt? You think I want to help the monsters who tore out my eye and then killed my mother? You have hated me since the second I stepped into the Ring. I don't know why, but you have."

"Stop!" roared the Fengo. "This is no time for squabbling."

Squabbling! Edme thought. *This wolf accuses me of being a turnpelt and he calls it squabbling!*

"Banja, I do believe you've lost your senses. If Edme doesn't go, how will Faolan find the Pit?" Finbar demanded.

"How do you know she will not lead Faolan into it and leave him there?"

There was a gasp. But before anyone could think or stop what happened next, it was as if a silver comet streaked through the *gadderheal.* Faolan leaped upon the red wolf and rolled her, her ruff firmly clamped in his jaws. He then held her down with both paws. "You know nothing! Edme is my dearest friend, and only a treacherous wolf would accuse her of such deceit." The other wolves were mute with shock.

"Off! Off! Faolan, now!" the Fengo ordered.

Faolan released his grip and backed away.

"Faolan! Banja! Listen to me," the Fengo commanded.

"Make her take it back," Faolan gasped.

"Don't act like a puppy who just lost at a game of *biliboo*." The Fengo wheeled around and then snapped at Banja. "Banja, you of all wolves should know better. What has gotten into you? Where is your dignity? You are a wolf of the Watch!" He was breathing heavily, as if this kind of outburst and the reprimand it demanded taxed him.

"Banja has had it out for Edme from the start," Faolan yowled.

"Stop whining!" The Fengo paused as if to catch his breath. "Now, both of you listen to me! The war is not in this *gadderheal*!" Finbar tossed his head toward the entrance. "It's out there. I will not tolerate such behavior. You go and make paw right — this instant!"

Paw right was the traditional gesture of making amends, setting disagreements aside, and reconciling with one's adversary. Each wolf was required to take three steps toward his or her opponent, then lift a paw and touch the other's paw lightly.

The two wolves approached each other as was prescribed. But when Faolan lifted his splayed paw, Banja made no move at all. Her eyes clamped onto the pad with the spiraling marks. She seemed transfixed and began to tremble.

"Banja!" the Fengo said sharply.

"I can't touch it, honorable Fengo."

"You can or you shall be *dalach'd*."

The wolf swallowed and finally lifted her paw and fleetingly touched Faolan's, then turned and stumbled away.

Faolan and Edme left immediately. Arthur flew overhead. He seemed like a different owl from the one Faolan had snatched out of the sky, mewling and frightened. It was as if he had grown up overnight, even acquired a slight measure of dignity. He took his job seriously, although he would not need to fly cover until they entered MacHeath territory. At the moment, Arthur was flying a quarter league ahead. But they saw him carve a turn and head back toward them as he sailed over a high ridge.

"He's flying fast!" Faolan observed. "What do you think he's found? Certainly not MacHeaths yet."

"No, not yet," Edme replied.

Arthur landed. "Bears, hundreds of them! You'll see them when you get to the top of the ridge."

"Oh, Great Ursus!" Faolan whispered at they scrambled up the shale slope. It was as if a dark ocean were rolling in from the west. He had no idea that there were so many bears in the Beyond. "They're marching on the Ring!"

"Let me find out," Arthur said. The Spotted Owl spread his wings and lifted into flight.

This is my chance, Arthur thought. *I'm tired of being bullied. Made fun of because of my wing tip.* Had he been born a wolf rather than an owl, he would have been flung from the nest. But Faolan and Edme had returned stronger, braver than ever. He wasn't sure if he had it in him to be really brave. Courage was a strange thing. For some, it came easy. But could there really be courage without fear? Was it courage that had made him take the dare to dive for the ember? Or was it something else — a poor imitation?

What had he hoped to gain? Respect? Glory? Not really. Just to be liked, accepted. How pitiful was that? Halfway through the prank, he began to realize how stupid it was. He had seen Faolan looking at him while he was cratering, and had begun to wonder if he could gather up his nerve to tell the wolves of the Watch about the cubnapping he'd witnessed. He'd been just about to fly down to Faolan's cairn, when suddenly that wolf was on him. He'd never seen a wolf jump so quicky or so high.

And what would he gain from his latest adventure? He wasn't sure, but he was certain that a war between the wolves and the bears would crack Faolan's gizzard. Of course, Arthur knew that Faolan didn't have a gizzard. . . . Marrow! That was it. The wolves were always swearing oaths by their marrow. But Arthur's own bones were hollow, so he swore by that organ most revered by owls. *By my gizzard, I must help stop this war!*

At that moment, Arthur knew he had crossed some invisible line. It was no longer simply about himself and his poor wing tip. His actions were on behalf of someone else and something larger than himself. There would be no glory, just hard work.

When Arthur drew close to the first line of bears, he swooped down low, swiveling his head one way, then another, to pick up conversation that might help. The words and language didn't differ that much among owls, bears, and wolves, but Arthur's ear was unaccustomed to the thick, rumbling brogue that ran through the bears' speech like the muffled roar of an underground river. He turned his head toward the southwest, and in the glimmering light of the dawn, he spotted the first of the wolves from the western Beyond approaching — a dark swagging line on the purpling horizon. "Great Glaux!" Arthur murmured. "They're coming from all over!"

Arthur was gone only briefly before Faolan and Edme saw him streaking his way toward them again.

"He came back," Edme said. "I thought he might fly away."

"He certainly had every chance to." Faolan paused. "But I had a hunch he wouldn't."

Arthur alighted on a flat rock, shoulder high to the wolves. "The bears are heading south and east. Toward the Black Glass Desert. It's their rallying point, and there are wolves going, too. Something about a *gaddergludder*. Not sure what that means."

Faolan and Edme looked at each other. "A rally — a wolves' rally before a hunt to raise the marrow and the taste for blood," Faolan replied.

"It's war," Edme said quietly.

"It must be. The Fengo and the *raghnaid* must . . . must . . ." He could barely utter the words. "Must have failed in their parley." The Fengo's voice echoed in their minds: *Words are cheap!*

"How long do the bears rally before they attack?" Edme asked.

"A day and a night, I think," Faolan answered. He tried to remember stories that Thunderheart had told him about bear rallies. But of course, there had never been a rally for a war with the wolves. They'd only been for small fights over territory.

Faolan had one thought: No war. He had one speed — attack speed, not press-paw. For Faolan, a war of sorts had already begun, a war between his wolf marrow and his bear heart. This was a war in which there would be no winners or losers. He would lose all, and win nothing.

So it was at attack speed that Faolan and Edme set out for the Pit, where the cub was held hostage by Old Cags. As they traveled, Edme explained as best she could about the peculiar torture chamber the MacHeaths had devised.

"I'm not sure why Old Cags never died of the foaming-mouth disease, but he didn't. The clan feeds on terror, brutality. Old Cags has become — how should I describe it? — their talisman, their charm, for young rebellious pups. They come out of the Pit with eyes like stone."

"Moon blinked," Arthur said.

"What?" Edme asked.

"Moon blinked. Before I was hatched, there was this bad place where some owls — bad owls — would take baby owls. It was called St. Aegolius Academy for Orphaned Owls. But the truth was, the owlets weren't orphaned, they were snatched. The bad owls took the babies to a place in the canyonlands that sounds a lot like the Pit. It was a deep, deep canyon, and they made the babies walk around at night under a blazing full moon. It did something to their brains. They couldn't think. They could only do what they were told."

"Moon blinked, you say," Faolan said. And he quickened his pace.

CHAPTER TWENTY-ONE

THE PIT

FAOLAN'S PLAN WAS TO RESCUE the cub and take him to the Black Glass Desert as quickly as possible. Surely, there was time. They had left shortly after midnight, and thankfully the wind was with them. At this speed, they could rescue the cub by the next dawn, and just possibly make it to the Black Glass Desert by evening.

Edme was intensely worried. Although she had never seen the Pit with Old Cags staggering about in it, she knew it was deep. Even though bears were much better climbers than wolves, it was said that the walls of the Pit were so sheer that climbing them was almost impossible.

There was a hidden trail in and out of the Pit, but how were they to find it? Old Cags's brains were such mush that he'd never found it in all the years he'd been there.

To add to all this was the problem of completing the rescue before war broke out between the wolves and the bears. Edme felt her marrow melt whenever she thought of it. But the anguish in Faolan's eyes was worse. She knew that to go to war with the bears would destroy Faolan in a way no foaming-mouth wolf or even the crushing blow of a grizzly bear could.

They traveled at attack speed as long as they could, then slowed to press-paw and ran on through the night. Just as the first rays of dawn peeped over the horizon, they arrived at the rim of the Pit. Faolan scrambled to the top of an outcropping and looked straight down. He saw the foaming-mouth wolf staggering along the east wall of the ravine, but there was no trace of the cub.

Then, after several anxious minutes, they saw a smudge of something emerge from the sheer rock wall. It was the cub.

"No name!" yelled the cub.

"Name!" screeched Old Cags and gathered himself to charge. But the little cub did not even flinch.

"Amazing," Edme whispered.

"It's a standoff." Arthur alighted on the outcropping. "I've been hovering here for a while. It's strange. There's a slot in the stone wall, just big enough for the cub to squeeze into."

"And not Old Cags?" Edme asked.

"I think he could if he was able to aim true for it. But you see how he staggers about. Something's wrong with the way he sees. But the strangest thing of all is how he keeps asking the cub his name. The cub won't tell. Just comes out and shouts, 'No name!' and this sets Old Cags off. The cub doesn't seem that scared. And every time he comes out, I can see that he's scanning the rock walls for the trail out." Arthur paused. "And I think I've found it."

"You have! Arthur!" Faolan exclaimed.

The Spotted Owl led them to a snarl of brambly bushes. "If you can slither under those on your bellies, a path widens out and then pitches almost straight down. Be careful."

"Let's think this out," Faolan said. "It might take us a bit of time to get down there. But once we do, we'll need to distract Old Cags."

"I can do that," Arthur quickly offered. "I can fly in. Go for a few kill spirals. Back loops. It'll drive him crazy."

"It's hard to think of him any crazier," Edme mused softly.

The trail was steep even for animals with four legs. They slid down the last part, causing a small avalanche of pebbles and loose rock. Old Cags heard this and came trotting over in anticipation of another pup or perhaps a bloody offering of fresh meat delivered by the wolves who worshipped him.

He stopped short and snarled as Faolan and Edme appeared. "Whazz name?"

Faolan and Edme were trembling. They had never been so close to a diseased animal, an animal with the foaming-mouth sickness. They split off in opposite directions as planned. Old Cags stood bewildered. He did not know which way to turn, and suddenly the wolves didn't seem to be wolves anymore. They were leaping and spinning in the air. For when Arthur had said he would distract the sick wolf with kill spirals, the two young Watch wolves immediately came up with the idea of running a series of scanning jumps. This they hoped would distract the wolf, and the less time they spent on the ground with Old Cags, the better.

The plan seemed simple. When the sick wolf's attention was sufficiently engaged, Faolan would race to the crack in the rock wall to fetch the cub while Edme and Arthur continued to distract Old Cags with jumps and fantastic flight maneuvers.

Old Cags's head was spinning as he tried to keep track of what appeared to be missiles of fur and feather streaking through the air. Faolan raced to the slot in the rock and stuck his head into the dim light. The damp shining eyes of a cub met his. Toby looked up, shocked. "Are you here to kill me? Drag me to Cags?"

"We're here to rescue you. Follow me. Be quick."

"You came for me?"

"Yes, quick now while Edme distracts Cags."

The two raced from the slot in the wall. The little cub looked up in time to see an owl dive straight down upon Cags and then see his old wolf playmate, Edme, leaping in somersaults.

"Edme!" Toby shouted. He couldn't help it. The name just burst out of him.

"Name!" shrieked Old Cags and swung his head in the direction of Edme. At last he had found his target — a real wolf.

CHAPTER TWENTY-TWO

DRUMS OF WAR

THERE WAS A FEELING OF UNREALITY as the Namara led an expeditionary force of one hundred MacNamara wolves south and west toward the Black Glass Desert, where the grizzlies of the Beyond had gathered for their drumming. The last war in the Beyond had been the War of the Ember, before the Namara had come of age and long before she was chieftain. Never had there been a war with the grizzlies. Was the world as she knew it falling apart? The seasons were all turned around, and now this threat of war. The Namara knew it had all started with the MacHeaths, for two she-wolves had fled to her and told her of a cub being snatched. For some dark reason that made sense only to twisted minds, the MacHeaths believed they would advance themselves by stealing a cub.

The Namara had brought the MacHeath she-wolves with her. The wolf Katria was an outflanker, and out-flankers were good in battle. She only wished the blind wolf Morag was healthy enough to fight as well. Morag's mate had generously offered his services, but if he were killed, who would care for the ailing Morag?

On their second day of traveling, while they were still far from the Black Glass Desert, a strange rumbling could be heard seeping up from the ground. They were traveling at half press-paw speed. Their hackles raised as the earth trembled beneath their paws.

The Namara howled the signal for a halt. She jumped up to a rock and eyed the troops of her clan. She was a wolf of middling size, with a pelt the color of storm clouds and vivid green eyes. She had a noble bearing, and the calmness of her demeanor concealed the turbulence of her feelings.

These are good wolves, she thought. More than half were she-wolves, but they could fight as ferociously as any male. In fact, she was now leading into battle the largest expeditionary force of she-wolves ever assembled. She had great confidence in her clan, and yet they'd never before gone against grizzlies. These wolves had honed their fighting skills on frequent skirmishes with the odi-ous MacHeaths.

Often, MacHeaths came to the far reaches of the Beyond in attempts to reclaim one of their deserters, and yet, never since the time of Hordweard had they succeeded. The Namara knew that in truth, it should be the MacHeaths they were fighting. But it was too late now. The MacHeaths had wreaked incalculable damage on the Beyond — on all its creatures — and now a war was coming. A messenger had come with the news that the first round of parleys had failed, and all clans were to report to the front. The grizzlies were not willing to talk; they were convinced that a sacred trust had been irrevocably broken. The wolves had no choice but to defend themselves or be destroyed by an enemy vastly larger and stronger than themselves.

Never had any wolf force gone up against the grizzly bears of the Beyond. And now this drumming, which was done expressly to stir fear and anguish in their marrow!

It was time for the Namara to address her troops.

"What you hear is not an earthquake. This is bear drumming, like our *gaddergludders* before a *byrrgis*. The purpose is to raise their blood thirst and to frighten us; that is all.

"Listen to me, wolves. I am not simple enough, not fool enough, to think you do not fear these bears. I fear them, too. But I am going to tell you something that might shock you. Our real enemy is not the bears."

There was a hush, and then the gathered wolves began to exclaim and murmur.

"No. It is not the bears we need to fight." Whispers began to rise, hackles stirred amid the Namara's troops. "We need to fight the cause of this heinous war, and the cause is the MacHeaths!" Utter silence now fell upon the Namara's troops. "The MacHeaths snatched an innocent bear cub, ripped him from his mother. And now if we do not stop the MacHeaths, the bears will attack, and we shall have no choice but to defend ourselves. So our first war is with the clan we know so well, through our blood and our history. We shall attack the MacHeaths. The MacNamaras, of all the wolves, know how to fight a MacHeath! And in fighting the MacHeaths, we can bring peace to the Beyond!

"Let me speak to you about fear. It is merely the other end of the bone of courage. One cannot exist without the other. Courage, as an ancient warrior once said, is fear holding on just a bit longer. We are fighting for our way of life in the Beyond, for which the first Fengo led us out of the Long Cold. It is worth the holding on, for believe me, it is better for us to fight for something than to live for nothing. We of the MacNamara clan do not trek into war with the jingle-jangle of the *tinulaba* of our bone necklaces. We do not go in for gewgaws, the decorations of rank, as other clans. For we are she-wolves and have no need of such trappings. We know who we are. We are the toughest frinking fighting force in the Beyond."

There was a great roar of howling from the troops, a roar as loud as the drumming of the grizzlies. The Namara signaled for quiet and continued. "If a she-wolf does her best, what else is there? No need for medals, or bones scraped up from the battlefield. And when those MacHeaths see us coming, they will raise their hind legs and wet in their own blasted fur, crying, 'Great Lupus, it's the frinking MacNamaras and that daughter of a she-wolf, the Namara herself!'"

The she-wolves went wild. The Namara's voice rose higher.

"And when this war is over, and you have a grandpup and she asks, 'What did you do in the great war against the bears?' you can look her straight in the eye and say, 'Daughter, your granny traveled with the great MacNamara expeditionary force and fought for justice alongside the toughest old she-wolf, Galana, the Namara of the clan!'"

CHAPTER TWENTY-THREE

"Edme! Edme! Edme!"

AFTER ALL THE TERRIFYING HOURS spent in the Pit never uttering his own name, Toby had shouted out the name of a friend. Soon the walls of the Pit were resounding with Old Cags bellowing, "Edme! Edme! Edme!" Long bubbly threads of foam inscribed the air as he advanced on Edme. She quit her jumping. Her intense green eye locked on Old Cags and began to grow dim. *It's turning to stone!* Faolan thought.

Not only had Edme seemed to freeze, with her eye so dim that it was now as blank as the missing one, as if it had become a void through which her marrow leaked out, but Old Cags seemed steady and focused. A new light burned in the diseased wolf's eyes, a glowing that spoke of his terror of dying diseased and alone. *He is frightened to die alone!* Faolan realized. *He wants to share his sickness and his final death!*

"Edme! Edme!" Old Cags chanted. "I need a name, I got a name, now nothing more will be the same. Edme, Edme, Edme! Come share the foam. We're not alone. Edme, Edme!" Old Cags was walking steadily, staggering no longer, and closing the distance between himself and a frozen Edme.

Arthur looked down. *Has the wolf gone yeep?* Yeep was a state in which an owl got so scared in midair that its wings locked, and the bird plummeted to the ground. And it looked as if the same thing had happened to the wolf. Edme stood stiff-legged and dazed as Old Cags advanced, screaming her name.

"Move! Edme! Run!" Faolan shouted.

It was as if she were ensnared in a terrible web that grew vaster as it reverberated with the din of her name, Edme, spinning through the Pit. The sticky threads of disease ensnared not just Edme but all of them.

Then the air seemed to split, the whining filaments of sound ripped apart as a blur of feathers bolted from above. Old Cags jerked, and then there was a terrible shriek — the alarm call of a Spotted Owl.

"Arthur!" Faolan let the name slip before he could stop himself.

"Arthur!" The sound was muffled, for Old Cags had a

firm grip on Arthur's port wing, which hung broken between his jaws.

"Run," Arthur cried. "Get the cub and run!"

They heard delicate owl bones crunching between Old Cags's jaws and saw blood dripping from his mouth. Edme raced to Faolan's side, where the cub huddled. They were still close to Old Cags, but the sick wolf was was so absorbed with his new partner in death that he paid them no heed. They watched the light fade in the Spotted Owl's eyes. Even the jewel-like sprinkling of white spots across the top of Arthur's head seemed to grow dull.

"Out!" Faolan ordered.

And the two wolves and the cub raced up the trail.

High above, on the edge of the rim, they looked down to the floor of the stone hell of the Pit as life expired in the brave young owl.

And it all began with a foolish dare, Faolan thought. There was a loud crack of thunder, and the sky splintered with lightning. And still they stayed as the Spotted Owl teetered on the threshold of death.

Toby looked up at the two wolves. He sensed they were in some deep trance as they watched their friend dying. The word the cub did not know was *lochinvyrr,* a death ritual that was instinctive among wolves. An urge flowed through them to acknowledge the dying animal's value.

The silent flyer will be gathered into the greater silence, Faolan thought. *Speed you to Glaumora now.* And he wondered if, as for wolves, the owls' Glaumora had a star ladder and a kindly spirit guide to help Arthur on his way. He looked toward the eastern horizon so bright with sun that the stars seemed far away, and then took one last look at Arthur. One wing was nearly torn off. *But surely there is a spirit owl who will help fly him to Glaumora, surely!* Faolan thought.

Now there was not much time.

Faolan knew that he and Edme must race with the cub to the Black Glass Desert, where the wolves and bears would battle. He had to get to the Fengo so the word could be spread that the cub was safe! Even from this vast distance, it seemed to him that he could hear reverberations of the drumming. *A day and a night . . . a day and a night.* That was how long Thunderheart said the bears massed. The very air seemed to throb with the sound of the pounding of the grizzlies' feet. There wasn't much time left now.

CHAPTER TWENTY-FOUR

THE BLACK GLASS DESERT

SOME CALLED IT THE DARKLANDS after the black sand made of glass fragments that absorbed nearly all light and reflected nothing. On this night, the blackness seemed to devour even the stars, the sliver of the newing moon, the threads of lightning that didn't flash or crackle but seemed to hang limply in the sky like gauzy cobwebs.

Faolan, Edme, and the cub stood on a cliff overlooking the desert, the rock beneath their feet trembling with the drumming of the bears. They could see the massive silhouettes of rank upon rank of bears. A gap of perhaps half a league separated the bears from the wolves, who were far greater in number but appeared, in comparison, like dwarf creatures.

Within Faolan a terrible war was already raging. *I am*

as much bear as wolf. How can one part of me lift a paw against the other?

He closed his eyes for a moment and pictured the spiraling lines on his pad — swirling in the night, like embers caught in the twisting hot drafts from a volcano's crater. He sometimes imagined that the spinning tracery that had marked him as a *malcadh* spoke of something not cursed but sublime. That the swirling design whispered of another pattern, a larger one of infinite harmony. Faolan knew that deep within him, two elements, bear and wolf, combined to make his essence, make him who he was. Now his marrow was turning bitter; to kill a bear was unthinkable. He raised a paw and gently stroked Toby's shoulder.

"I can't see my mum from here. It's too dark." Toby had flattened himself on the ground and was hanging his head over the edge of the cliff to peer out into the blackness.

"We'll find her, dear," Edme said consolingly.

How are we going to do this? Faolan thought. There were hundreds of bears out there, maybe thousands, and in the thickening darkness they all looked like one big mass.

There was an awkward fluttering in the air above them. It was an owl, and she was furious.

"Gwynneth!" Faolan shouted.

"Are you *yoicks?*" she spluttered. "Numbskulls! You're supposed to be back on your cairns at the Ring. You're going to get in big —" Gwynneth stopped abruptly. "Who's that?" she asked, looking at Toby.

"I'm a cub. And I don't like the way you talk to my friends, stupid!"

"Now, now, dear." Edme butted Toby gently on the neck. "She doesn't understand."

"I certainly don't," Gwynneth said. She looked dumbfounded for a moment, but then a light sparkled in her black eyes. "No! The cub!" She gasped. "You're the missing cub!"

"I certainly am!" Toby growled.

Faolan stepped forward to where the owl perched. "This is Toby. The MacHeaths snatched him and put him in the Pit."

"The Pit!" Gwynneth murmured. "Great Glaux, I thought the Pit was just a rumor — such a horrifying one that every owl is frightened even to fly over it. A foaming-mouth wolf! How did he survive —"

"They rescued me!" Toby shouted. Gwynneth's beak dropped open with astonishment. "And you called them numbskulls!" Toby growled low and deep. It was such a mature growl, it surprised all of them.

"Calm down, Toby. Gwynneth meant no harm. She didn't understand. She's one of my oldest friends in the Beyond," Faolan soothed.

"How can she be your good friend if I am?" Toby began to whine, sounding once again like an immature cub.

Edme put her muzzle right in front of Toby's brown eyes. "Faolan has a large, generous heart. He can be a good friend to many. Now, let's end this nonsense and figure out how to get you back with your mum and stop this disastrous war!" Edme turned to Gwynneth. "Gwynneth, will you fly back to the Fengo and tell him we have the cub? The word must be spread as fast as possible."

The two wolves felt the brush of a soft wind gust and the next thing they knew, Gwynneth was soaring above them.

As the owl flew in and was seen to perch on Grizz's massive shoulder, the drumming seemed to pause. Grizz was the grizzly elder known also as the Bear of Bears of the Beyond. Although the social organization of the bears was not nearly as structured as that of the wolves, the Bear of Bears was a kind of chieftain. He settled territorial disputes between bears and dealt with all business transacted between the wolves and the bears of the Beyond. Grizz was very old at this point and, despite his size, he was weak. Palsied, blind in one eye, with only dim vision in the other, and with many of his teeth missing, Grizz was clearly not long for this earth. His paw shook uncontrollably as the owl whispered in his ear.

"You say Toby's been found?" he rasped. "My great-grandson's been found!"

"Yes," Gwynneth replied. "He comes now with an escort assigned by the Fengo."

"Bring him forth and we shall parley with the wolves."

"What? Impossible!" Dunbar MacHeath stared at his scout. "You're sure, Fretta?"

"I'm sure. The cub has been rescued."

"Who? Who rescued him?"

"Edme and the wolf Faolan."

Dunbar MacHeath's scar quivered like a boiling river running down his clenched face. "This . . . this . . ." His voice was ragged.

The MacHeath lieutenants regarded Dunbar nervously. They'd never seen him like this before.

"Why are you looking at me so stupidly?" Dunbar snarled. "You idiots. This will be our undoing. With the cub rescued, there's no chance for a war with the bears. We're finished." He paused and his eyes rolled up until only the barest crescent of green showed against the whites. "Unless . . ." he began slowly.

"Unless what, Lord Chieftain?" Malan asked.

Dunbar MacHeath wheeled around to Fretta. "Where is the cub now? Where's Grizz?"

"Top lieutenants from the Watch have met up with Edme and Faolan. They're escorting the cub to the center of the Black Glass Desert, to the Twisted Four-four."

"You mean the four *yondos* in the middle of the desert?"

"Yes. Grizz is making his way now to the Fengo for a parley at those *yondos*, not far from where the bears have assembled for their rally. The cub is to be delivered directly to Grizz."

"Grizz is old and unsteady!" Dunbar MacHeath said, his ears shoved forward and his hackles raised. "He's a perfect target for a *slink melf*!"

"Aaaah!" An exhalation of relief and hope reverberated through the cave.

"There will be a war yet with the bears. Malan, Fretta,

Blyden, Andreen, Aila, Donaidh! We go now. Attack speed! By my marrow, the Sacred Ring shall be ours!"

A savage howling erupted from the gathered wolves as the largest *slink melf* ever assembled tore out of the cave and streaked toward the four *yondos* on the darkling plains of the Black Glass Desert.

With the exception of the MacHeaths, there had been much rejoicing among the clans of the Beyond when Toby returned unharmed. What had initially begun as a march to the opening front of a terrible war was now a joyous journey to celebrate the return of a cub. There were two wolves, however, whose relief was tinged with anxiety.

"You know what this means?" Katria said in a low voice to Airmead.

The white wolf nodded. "Yes, of course. Dunbar MacHeath will not go silently into oblivion."

The two wolves stopped as the rest of the MacNamaras flowed by them.

"He'll still want his war," Katria said. "They'll be up to something."

Without saying another word, Katria and Airmead peeled off from the expeditionary force and headed toward the rondos in the Black Glass Desert, intent on stopping any wolves who wanted to turn the celebration into a bloodbath.

Airmead marveled that soon Katria, hackles raised and nose to the ground, began picking up not just scents but tracks — tracks that, to another wolf, might seem anonymous. But Katria knew these paw prints from when she had to press the wolves running a *byrrgis* into crimping maneuvers, blocking strategies, and tackling sprints. She had run nearly every position on a MacHeath *byrrgis*. "This is Blyden . . . and of course Donaidh — the old fool. I'd know his paw print anyplace. And here's Malan and Fretta." She stopped in her tracks. "Andreen! Aila! Great Lupus! It's a *slink melf* led by Dunbar!" She looked up at Airmead. "They're going to assassinate Grizz!"

A large silence opened up in the Darklands, like jaws that seemed to swallow the drumming of the bears in anticipation of the cub's arrival. It was as if the entire Beyond had paused to savor the momentous event. Wolves shoved their ears forward, owls rotated their heads so their ear slits could catch the rumbled whispers that began to rise from the army of bears. "They say he's coming. Toby is coming!"

Then near the Twisted Four, a voice split the drumming. "Toby!" Bronka roared. The mother and cub ran toward each other through a dark, winding path that wove between the small hillocks, separating the four *yondos*. Grizz roared in jubilation.

"Where are they?" Airmead said desperately. The track for the *slink melf* had gone cold almost as soon as they had reached the Black Glass Desert. Unlike dirt, the granules of the fine sand could not hold a print. The *slink melf*'s scent, too, seemed to evaporate in the dry air.

"We have to keep our eyes on Grizz," Airmead said.

"You watch Grizz. I'll watch the dark." Katria had begun to realize that the Black Glass Desert was not all dark in the same way. And although the eerie dunes and plains seemed shadowless, there were more shades of black than one might imagine. Katria caught a movement at the far edge of her vision, less than forty strides away, where Grizz had just turned behind one of the hillocks.

An extraordinary energy coursed through her. She had no memory of her feet leaving the ground, but suddenly she was airborne and sailing over the small hill that obscured Grizz. Her teeth sank into Andreen's ruff just as Andreen sank her teeth into the haunches of the Bear of Bears. There was a roar that sounded as if the earth were being torn apart. Katria, her vision obscured by spraying blood, somehow managed to jump clear as Grizz's massive body began to collapse.

There was a thunderous howling followed by the rumbling growls of bears. "Grizz was attacked!" someone yelled. And that someone was not Grizz's guards but Dunbar MacHeath himself! The *slink melf* had managed to vanish except for Andreen, who was pinned under the Grizz's body. A tangle of wolves surrounded Edme. She glimpsed Jasper and the Fengo, but there were others.

It took Edme a split second to understand what had transpired. "It's the MacHeaths! They attacked."

"No!" Dunbar started to shout as he raced away from where the *slink melf* had been. He didn't get far before Edme was upon him like an airborne missile. She tore open his face, ripping the scar that her own mother had carved. She pulled and pulled on his flesh, digging her fangs in ever deeper until she sliced into the life-giving artery in his neck and a huge spurt of blood drenched her.

Dunbar MacHeath looked at her with bewilderment. "How? How?" he gurgled.

"I finished my mum's work, that's all," Edme whispered.

"Death to the wolves," someone from the throng of bears cried out. "Death to the wolves."

"No!" roared a she-bear. It was Toby's mum. She loped forward with both her cubs riding on her back. "Listen to me! Listen!"

"It's Bronka. Bronka and both her cubs," others whispered.

The Bear of Bears stirred. The throngs gathered closer as they watched him stagger to his feet. Crushed beneath him was the body of Andreen.

"Who is this wolf?" Grizz asked, somewhat dazed.

Edme stepped forward. "She's Andreen MacHeath, point wolf for the MacHeath clan's assassination operations."

"Did you kill her?" the Bear of Bears roared.

"Not me." Edme turned her head to look for Katria.

"I did," said Katria, stepping out from behind a *yondo*. "I'm Katria, former outflanker of the MacHeath clan, now a member of the noble MacNamaras."

"You saved my life," said the Bear of Bears, and began to bow down to her painfully on his arthritic knees, though even bowed, he stood twice as high as the black-as-night wolf. "You saved my life," he repeated.

"I did, but there are two wolves who saved many lives," Katria said.

"Wh-what . . ." Grizz stammered softly. It was as if his mouth could not form the words.

"Edme, the wolf who killed the MacHeath chieftain, and the other, the silver wolf. These two found the cub and brought them here to stop a war that should never have started."

"Yes, yes," the Bear of Bears said softly, marveling at the wonder of it all.

The Fengo now made his way up to where the Bear of Bears knelt.

"Honorable Grizz, Bear of Bears, the peace that has reigned in the Beyond for over a thousand years was nearly destroyed by the brutality of one clan."

He looked toward the MacHeaths. Dunbar and Andreen were dead. Donaidh had escaped, but Malan and Fretta had been rounded up. "As Fengo of the Watch, I now invoke the privilege accorded only to myself, the privilege of the Supreme Sayer. On occasions of great peril, it is my right to dispense with a Court of *Crait* and issue an immediate pronouncement — a *Fengasso*, or last word of the Fengo. I hereby declare that the MacHeaths are no longer a clan of the wolves of the Beyond." Malan and Fretta's eyes flashed green in the night as they looked at each other. *Was it regret, remorse, or was there the glint of a challenge?* Edme wondered.

"From this moment hence, they are outclanners and shall be treated as such. Nevermore will their gnaw wolves be permitted to participate in the *gaddergnaw* competitions for selection to the Watch. Nor will they be permitted to attend the moon celebrations of the longest night, when all the clans gather. Nor will they be permitted to join with packs of other clans for *byrrgises*. I shall ask the Namara to dispatch a patrol from her clan to chase the MacHeaths from the Beyond into the Outermost immediately. From this moment, they are *crait*!"

CHAPTER TWENTY-FIVE

EIGHT MOONS PASSING

THE MOON OF THE FLIES HAD come and gone, along with the Moon of the Mossflowers and the Caribou Moon, followed by the three winter moons. The odd thing was that, although the sun still rose and fell according to the seasons and the days were growing longer now, the rivers were still frozen. It was the Moon of the Cracking Ice, but snow still lay thick on the ground. Faolan and Edme were nearing the completion of their first year on the Watch of the Ring. They had now perched on every cairn that overlooked each of the five volcanoes. They had learned the volcanoes' temperaments and how their moods changed through a moon from first shine to no shine, when the moon vanished. They knew the smell of each volcanoes' sulfurous expulsions. They knew that the most boring watch was on Kiel, a shield volcano whose long, gently sloping lava flows yielded the fewest retrievable coals and therefore was the least visited by colliering owls.

One evening early in the Moon of the Cracking Ice, Faolan stood perched on a cairn overlooking Dunmore. He had just completed a series of scanning jumps off the keybone when he looked down and saw a wolf trotting toward him. An unmistakable wolf, the Sark of the Slough.

She was a freakish creature with eyes of different colors — one the true green of a wolf of the Beyond, the other an amberish gold that skittered about without any seeming focus. Her pelt blew like a She-Wind in raging disorder about her bony frame, so she looked like a small approaching weather front. Icicles had formed on the fur beneath her jaw so it seemed as if she had a long, glistening beard, which added to the strangeness of her appearance. But along with Gwynneth and Edme, the Sark was one of Faolan's closest friends in the Beyond.

She looked up at Faolan and said, "Come with me."

"I can't. I'm on watch," Faolan answered.

"I've arranged it with the Fengo," the Sark replied. And sure enough, Faolan saw Twistling trotting toward the cairn.

"Go along now, young'un. You got business to do with the Sark. I'll take this shift and have arranged to cover the rest while you're gone."

Business? Faolan was completely confused and suddenly apprehensive. A quiver ran through his marrow.

Before the moon had risen to wolf's peak, they were well on their way. The Sark had set a course due north, but now they had begun to veer to the east. She hadn't spoken since they left, not a word about their destination or why she was taking him to it. He knew better than to ask. Unnecessary questions made the Sark incredibly cranky, and a cranky Sark was not one that any wolf wanted to deal with. A Masked Owl suddenly appeared overhead.

"Gwynneth!" Faolan howled. But she merely looked down and gave him an intensely somber look. The quiver that had coursed through his marrow quieted and was replaced with a strange and deep longing. He quickened his pace.

"Slow down," the Sark said gently. "Don't wear yourself out. We'll get there in time."

In time for what? he wondered. He thought he noticed a glimmering in the Sark's steady eye, a tear. Gwynneth swooped down to fly low, and Faolan felt a quiet shudder of air as she hovered over him. It seemed to Faolan as if he were folded into the shadow of her wings, as if she were tying to protect him. For the next day and a half, they traveled this way, making only brief stops for rest. Faolan had never been so far north. It was in the late afternoon with the sun still bright on the horizon that he realized they were crossing the top of a peninsula.

"We're going to the MacNamara clan, aren't we?" Faolan said.

The Sark stopped. The snow was up to her belly. Gwynneth lighted down on a snow-covered rock and spread her talons wide to support her weight so that she didn't sink into the powder. Faolan looked at the two creatures regarding him with tear-filled eyes. "Would you two like to tell me what this is about?"

"Fao-lan." The Sark's voice cracked. She began again. "Faolan, we're taking you to meet your first Milk Giver."

The Namara herself came out to greet them and lead them to a den at the edge of the encampment. "She's waiting. Brangwen thought it best that we not tell her yet." The Namara turned to Faolan, who was still reeling with astonishment and had not uttered a word since being told. "You mother, your first Milk Giver, is dying. She's blind, so she might not know you."

"Oh, but she will! SHE WILL!" he replied fiercely.

"Come, young'un." A large, handsome red wolf appeared beside Faolan. "I am your mother's second mate, Brangwen MacDonegal. Follow me."

The den was a small west-facing cave flush with the low-angled afternoon sun. On a pile of thick elk skins lay a frail but once beautiful silver wolf. As soon as they entered the cave, Morag's nostrils began to twitch. She lifted her head from the pelt, but just barely. "Who is this? Who comes?"

No one spoke a word as Faolan crawled on his belly toward his first Milk Giver. He tipped his muzzle so she could sniff him. Tears began to stream from her filmed eyes. "Is it? Is it really you?" she asked.

Faolan lifted his splayed paw and pressed it gently to Morag's mouth. She knew instinctively what he wanted. Her tongue slipped out and began to lick the spiraling marks on the pad of his paw.

"Great Lupus, I am blessed! You survived! You survived! I thought so when I found the bones of the grizzly. What was it, ten moons after your birth? I smelled you on those bones. I had hoped, I had prayed. But now I know it's true. The blessed grizzly gave you her milk. I smell that, too, even now."

"Yes, Mum. I survived. Thunderheart made me grow. I am a wolf of the Watch now."

"The Watch!" she exclaimed as tears streamed from her sightless eyes and she began to lick his face. "Thunderheart was the name of your second Milk Giver?"

"Yes, Mum."

He nestled closer to her until he could feel the beat of her heart, its strange rhythms as it sped up, then seemed to falter. He closed his eyes and listened as he rested his face against her shoulders. Her breathing grew ragged.

"And what do they call you?" she gasped.

"Faolan. Thunderheart named me Faolan. It means 'gift from the river.'"

"Gift," she murmured. "I had planned to name you Skaarsgard after the Star Wolf, who helps spirits climb the star ladder to the Cave of Souls."

"Why?" Faolan asked.

"Because although your pelt was not yet thick, I could tell it was silvery and it looked as if the stars had fallen into it. But Faolan, that is a lovely name. Gift, yes. That's a perfect name, for I felt blessed when you were born. You were not cursed in the least. You were my gift and they took my gift away. . . . Gift . . ." she whispered, her voice growing dimmer. "Gift," she said, her tongue still on his paw. Once more she said the word, barely audibly, then Faolan felt the last beat of her heart.

He lay there for a while. But soon the warmth began to seep out of her body, and he knew that he must go out into the cold for the last part of his *Slaan Leat*, a final part of the journey he would never have anticipated ten moons ago.

Epilogue

HE TRAVELED ALONE TO THE END of the peninsula, an icy point that jutted out into the raging Sea of Hoolemere. It was here that he had decided to build the *drumlyn* for his mother, Morag, with bones he'd found buried in the snow along the way.

The Sark and Gwynneth said they would wait for him. "No matter how long it takes," the Sark said. "And in the summer, if ever there is a summer again, you can come back and add her bones to the *drumlyn.*"

Faolan found a rough shelter in the lee of the point and set about incising the bones. He would add more, including some from his first Milk Giver, as the years passed. Perhaps soon the huge skeleton of Thunderheart might break apart, and he could carry one to this point. But he would not worry about that now. A small *drumlyn* was better than no *drumlyn*. He began his carving with what he thought might have been his first memories — those of the other wriggling pups beside him, their scent. He only remembered their scent for, as a newborn, his eyes were sealed shut and he would not have known the other pups by sight. The sensations of those first days came back to him one by one. Many of them were feelings of absence — the absence of the wriggling movement; the void of scent; the lack of warmth. Then these vacancies were filled with something unbearably cold — the sterile smell of what he presumed must have been the Obea.

After a full night of carving, Faolan looked at the bones and realized that, although he had carved them eloquently, he had very little to say. In comparison to the bones he had carved for Thunderheart's *drumlyn*, these seemed empty. But he knew so little about his first Milk Giver in comparison to Thunderheart. He was not sure what to carve next. From the first moment he entered the den where she lay dying, he knew he loved her. It seemed in a strange way as if he had never left her. Her pelt was familiar although much less lustrous than it must have once been. He had loved the feeling of her tongue tracing the spirals on his splayed paw. It was so alive, so intimate, so motherly. *I have a mum.* The words streamed through his mind. And so that was what he carved, over and over until it became *I have two mums. I grew with the milk of two mums in my blood. The milk of two in my marrow.*

A blizzard had been blowing for the two days Faolan carved, but on the night of the second day, as he began to build the small *drumlyn*, the snow began to fall more slowly. The wind ceased and each flake appeared like a jewel against the blackness of the night. The Great Star Wolf had just begun to climb out of its winter den on the other side of the earth to appear in the eastern sky along with the ladder to the Cave of Souls. Faolan howled as he built the *drumlyn*. It was the howling known as *glaffling*, the howl of grief and mourning. But as he placed the last bone and looked up, he saw something astonishing. The mist of Morag was shimmering in the sky, and then not far behind it was a larger mist, an immense vaporous shape that loomed at the base of the star ladder and followed his first Milk Giver. It was his second Milk Giver. It was Thunderheart! Finally, she had sprung from the *drumlyn* he had made by the river. Finally, she had left the earth. Finally, she knew he had grown up safely and she could look down at him from Ursulana!

His *glaffling* turned to joy. He began to howl louder

than ever. How often had he looked at the spiraling lines on his paw and felt as if they marked a larger pattern, a larger plan, one of endlessly swirling harmonies like the movement of the stars. For they, too, were part of something larger as the sky turned around the earth. Of all this, Faolan howled.

The Sark and Gwynneth, waiting for him at least two leagues away, turned to each other. "What is he howling?" Gwynneth asked.

"Ursulana, the Cave of Souls. Two heavens are one," the Sark replied softly to the Masked Owl.

So sayeth Faolan, Watch wolf of the Ring.

AUTHOR'S NOTE

THE AUTHOR WISHES TO ACKNOWL-
edge that the Namara's speech in Chapter 22, "Drums
of War," is based largely on General George S. Patton's
speech to the American Third Army, Sixth Armored
Division, on May 31, 1944, in England shortly before the
Allied invasion of Normandy.